HAIR-TRIGGER

HAIR-TRIGGER

a novel by

TREVOR CLARK

CANADA

Library and Archives Canada Cataloguing in Publication

Clark, Trevor, 1955–, author
Hair-trigger / Trevor Clark.

ISBN 978–1–926942–62–9 (pbk.)

I. Title.

PS8555.L373H35 2014   C813'.54   C2013–906593–8

Printed and bound in Canada on 100% recycled paper.

Now Or Never Publishing
#313, 1255 Seymour Street
Vancouver, British Columbia
Canada V6B 0H1

nonpublishing.com
Fighting Words.

We acknowledge the support of the Canada Council
for the Arts for our publishing program.

To Julia, *mon joli chat*, claws and all,
and to Patrick, RIP—inspiration for one of
the sparkling characters in these pages, before
coke put him under the ground.

"He saw a man who appeared to be on the verge of death stagger into a movie theatre that was showing a picture called *Blonde Beauty*. He saw a ragged woman with an enormous goiter pick a love story magazine out of the garbage can and seem very excited by her find."

~Nathaniel West,
Miss Lonelyhearts

"Louis had never been in combat either. No, but he'd seen two men shot—one running from a work gang at Huntsville, another climbing the fence at Starke— and had seen a man stabbed to death, a man set on fire, a man right after he'd been strangled with a coat hanger, and believed these counted for something."

~Elmore Leonard,
Rum Punch

" 'Sickness is not only in body, but in that part used to be call: soul. Poor your friend he spend his money on earth in such continuous tragedies.' "

~Malcolm Lowry,
Under The Volcano

I

He couldn't draw on the roach anymore, so Rowe finished his drink and decided he was ready for the bars. His telephone rang while he was in the washroom, but he was too high to risk a complicated conversation while trying to get out the door. After the third ring, however, it was apparent that the machine wasn't on. Flushing the toilet, he zipped up on his way to the living room and answered it.

"Is Derek Rowe there?"

"Yeah . . . speaking."

"This is Detective Myers, Fifty-Two Division. Do you know a John Malone?"

This brought him down somewhat. "No."

"You don't? You don't know a John Malone?"

Rowe tried to concentrate. Why did that name sound familiar? It occurred to him that it probably had something to do with Lofton, an alias or something he'd once said he'd used. Earlier, when he'd dropped in at work, Lofton had mumbled something about planning to shoplift a bottle of vodka on his way home. "Oh . . . wait," Rowe said slowly. "I think I know who you mean. It's just that I know him as Jack, not John, and I don't know his last name. Why?"

"Well, let's make sure we're talking about the same individual. Is he a heavy-built guy with a bit of a beard and tattoos?"

Lofton had given them his number, so presumably he wanted Rowe to ID him. Now he was supposed to negotiate fact from fiction, half-wasted. "Yeah, he's got a barbed wire thing around his biceps."

"And zigzagging like lightning bolts on the insides of his arms?"

"Yeah, that's him."

"What's his first name?"

"Well, you know, Jack. John. I used to work with him and never really knew his last name, but Malone sounds like it. It's the same guy. I can vouch for him." Rowe listened to himself talk from a distance. He seemed to be enunciating clearly. "As far as I know, he doesn't have a record."

"Where does he live?"

"I don't know exactly. Just that it's around Harbord and Bathurst."

"Do you have his phone number?"

"No . . . I think it's in the book."

The detective used a different tone—confidential, on the level: "Okay—now what's his *real* name?"

Rowe was having difficulty with the conversation, which was fucking up his mood. "As far as I know, that is his real name, like I think I was saying. I've known him for years. He's all right, I can vouch for him, but he's been drinking a lot because his divorce just came through and he's been taking it hard. So . . . if there's anything I can do to help him out, let me know."

After he managed to get off the phone, he realized that he didn't know what Lofton had been arrested for exactly. This cop Myers probably wouldn't have told him anyway since he didn't seem to believe him, and they liked to be the ones asking the questions.

It looked like there was time for another drink before heading out.

Rowe decided to take the subway to avoid a second DUI, and left his rusting Firebird among the more affluent cars on St. Clair. While he waited for the light to change, a Union Jack flapped lazily over the door of a home across the street. In the neighbouring park there were sculptures by two long-dead female artists, whose nearby house, visible from his kitchen window, was now closed and marked by an historic plaque.

He crossed the intersection and walked west toward Yonge, noticing a pair of raccoons on the north side ambling along the floodlit lawn of Our Lady of Perpetual Help. While Rowe paused on the bridge to light a cigarette, he wondered at the glow circling the moon. A few stars twinkled. Between the treetops in the ravine below, two white lights on a smoke-stack down near the lake shore blinked, while to the left, where the valley cut southeast, cars back on Mount Pleasant appeared to be driving through the forest.

At the bank, Rowe stood in a foyer between the heavy glass doors and worked the machine. A view on the monitor from the security camera mounted near the ceiling behind him revealed a dazzling line of scalp where he used to part his hair, which was now greying and cropped short. He turned his head, checking his profile, and straightened up as he flexed his shoulders to emphasize the musculature of a still-lean physique.

Lately it felt as if there was nowhere to go but down. After a string of no-account jobs and a record for assault, cocaine possession and drunk driving, he'd risked what little he had by robbing two banks. Rowe had also begun to ponder the fact that at forty-four he had never married or been in much dan-ger of it, though he suspected that there was a child some-where. Women of any quality were getting harder to come by. The last female he could take any real pride in was a twenty-three-year-old he'd met at a dance in Chinatown in the spring, who'd marvelled that he was as old as Uncle. If he was ever to be with anyone that young again he'd more than likely be pay-ing for it.

The small bookstore he managed didn't provide a pension plan, drug or medical benefits, and twenty-seven grand a year left little to save towards retirement. That meant that he was going to end up living in a box beneath an underpass. Coming to terms with this some months earlier, he'd gone beyond skimming from the till to buying a prop beard, wrap-around shades and a Blue Jays cap, and robbing a Scotiabank and CIBC with nothing more than a note. The second teller gave him a dye grenade which exploded in his stolen car.

Glancing at the monitor again, he punched a few more buttons and collected his debit card, cash and receipt.

After a drink at the Hard Rock Café, Rowe found himself at Yonge and Dundas leaning against the Currencies International window under a row of florescent tubing. He watched people walking by. Handbills were plastered to a dirty metal garbage bin by the streetcar stop. There was a pawnshop, a cheque-cashing operation, and an arcade nearby whose pinball sign was missing letters. To the east by the steps down into the subway some blacks were talking outside Mr. Jerk Caribbean take-out; a panhandler with a ripped cardboard box was sitting in front of the World's Biggest Jean Store across the street. Almost everyone walking past looked slightly off. While alcohol served to beautify the world, Rowe found that marijuana tended to zero in on every conceivable ugliness with an accompanying sense of detachment.

"Got a cigarette?" A woman with straggly blondish hair was suddenly standing in front of him. Rowe reached into his pocket. When he struck a match for her, he checked out her weathered face in the stark lighting: her complexion was pockmarked and her blue eyes devoid of flirtation, hostility, a spark of anything, really. She was wearing a denim jacket over a pink sweatshirt, cotton-type slacks, sneakers, no socks. He figured her for thirty-eight, thirty-nine, and thought she was going to ask for spare change as she exhaled, squinting at him. "I'll give you a fuck for forty bucks, or a blowjob for twenty."

"No. No thanks, I'm all right."

"Twenty then."

"Can't afford it."

"How much do you have?"

He found he was enjoying the exchange, but knew she was going to have to be discouraged. "Ten bucks."

"All right. Ten bucks for a blowjob."

"No," he bluffed, "ten bucks for a fuck."

The woman looked at him through narrowed eyes, and took a drag. "Okay, let's go."

Rowe wasn't sure what to say. They were at a downtown intersection. He followed her a few doors east, wondering where she was going, when she turned to him at the entrance of an alley. "I need the money now."

Opening his wallet, he was surprised to see that he really did only have ten dollars. Fuck. Looked like he was wasted enough to have deposited his pay cheque and then forgotten to take out any money. "Listen, I've been drinking quite a bit tonight, so to be honest we're probably not going to have sex. I'll give you five bucks right now, and if anything happens I'll give you the other five."

"No, man—"

"Listen for a second. I'll smoke some dope with you, we'll have a nice little chat, you'll get five dollars for nothing, and that'll probably be it. On the off chance anything happens, you'll get another five. You can't lose," he said, holding out the bill.

She hesitated, and then took it.

The lane ran north behind some buildings along Yonge Street. In the dim light a large rat scurried across the stained pavement, which was littered with trash. About forty feet from the street she led him into a doorway that reeked of urine by some overflowing garbage cans, and tossed away her cigarette. Rowe looked around as he took a joint from his wallet and unwrapped the aluminum foil, kneeling gingerly on the stoop for a perspective level with her crotch. He couldn't foresee needing the condom in his wallet. "Where are you from?" he asked, lighting up.

"Pembroke Street."

Holding his breath, Rowe passed it to her, trying to overlook their lack of privacy. Anyone could walk by. As he exhaled, he said, "Listen, why don't you pull down your pants?"

She handed the joint back. Hooking her thumbs in the elasticized waist with her back against the metal door, she drew them down with her panties and stood with her legs slightly parted. Taking another toke, he looked at her flat stomach and studied her pussy in the light brown hair, touching her with his left hand and opening her labia. Awkwardly, he pulled down his jeans.

Ten seconds later she said, "Car," and yanked up her slacks.

Rowe, still kneeling, was partially erect as headlights lit up the side of the doorway. A police cruiser pulled up behind him. Ah, a new fucking low. He flicked his joint into the corner and looked over his shoulder, unsure if his bare ass was covered by the thin coat.

The cop at the wheel studied him. "Are you proposing?"

He didn't know whether or not to laugh. "Yeah, she's quite the catch."

"He just came in here to take a pee," she said.

That seemed impressive. "Yeah, I had to take a pee."

The policeman looked from one to the other, frowning. "Well, time to move on."

Rowe tried to pull up his pants discreetly as he got to his feet. Zipping himself up as he stepped past the car, he said, "Thanks."

At Dundas, he noticed that the alley had an actual street sign: O'Keefe Lane. He looked back at the cruiser, still parked behind them in the relative darkness near the rear of Harvey's restaurant, and put his hands in his pockets as he turned to the woman. "So, is that it?"

"Yeah."

"All right," he said. "Well, see you."

She started walking east. He looked around for a bank machine as he went back to the corner.

2

The holding cell had a bench, cement floor, steel door, no window. The detective came on tough. "Okay," he said, "that's not your real name. What's your real name? What's your address?"

Jack Lofton looked up at him. "John Malone, like I told the police who arrested me. Thirty-three Rosedale, apartment fifteen-fifteen."

The moustache and military haircut didn't buy it, but he went away.

Lofton had been grabbed by a security guard outside Canadian Tire for shoplifting a hunting knife. He hadn't hit him on the assumption that the police were on their way and he'd be fighting an assault charge too, which was a mistake since he'd ended up having to make conversation with the guard for over two hours in the basement of the store while they waited for the law to show. When he went to the washroom he slipped his only piece of ID, a plastic library card, inside the torn lining of his black leather jacket.

While they drove along Dundas Street W., one of the two arresting officers told him, "Look, I *know* you're lying to me. Don't make me have to bring in the detectives and start an investigation."

Once inside the station they went through his pockets and confiscated his cigarettes, checked his jacket and even his bandanna. Although there were no cards or licenses in his wallet, they found a paper with phone numbers on it and might have made some calls. The cop who seemed to be working in tandem with the detective came back into the cell and said,

"Okay, you've got two choices. There's no way we're going to put you in jail with all these spikes on your shoulders. Now, we can cut the epaulets off, or you and I can sit here with screwdrivers and take them off."

"I guess I like the second choice."

"I thought you would."

As they worked, Lofton had asked, "Do you mind if I smoke?"

"I don't give a fuck."

"Um, you wouldn't happen to have a cigarette, would you?"

The big walleyed cop gave him one, then went outside and found a pair of pliers when one of the steel studs wouldn't unscrew.

Now the detective was back. "What's your address again?"

"Thirty-three Rosedale. Apartment fifteen-fifteen."

"You're lying. We just called that building. The floors only go up to twelve, so there's no *way* you live in fifteen-fifteen. If you don't tell us the truth you're going to be charged with obstructing justice on top of whatever outstanding warrants you probably have. You're getting into deeper shit every minute."

After he left, Lofton looked at his watch. It was going on ten-thirty. Aside from an armed robbery charge that was thrown out in California, he'd managed to sidestep legal trouble throughout most of his life. This recent string of fuck-ups was a bad joke.

Though he'd been trying to appear affable or at least convey an impression of good faith, he knew his pale eyes had an unfriendly cast, even in repose. Not to mention the scrapes on his face from an altercation he barely remembered after waking up drunk behind a dumpster two nights earlier.

Just past eleven-thirty, they let Lofton use the phone on the wall outside the cell. Detectives in the large room were sitting at desks questioning suspects and typing reports. He called

Derek Rowe, and not knowing if he was being taped, left a message simply saying that he'd been arrested and needed him to stand up for him in court at the Old City Hall the next morning at nine. He gave him the room number and added, "You have to do this for me, man. It's very, *very* important."

They had met a decade earlier at a singles bar near Yonge and Eglinton where he'd been working security and Rowe was a regular who thrived in that meat market scene. There had been years of drinking together since, and the guy had money.

Later, the cop took him downstairs to have him booked. They fingerprinted him and stood him in front of a computer camera which processed his image into a data bank. At that point the arresting officer said, "Listen, let's have another look at that jacket of yours." Lofton took it off and handed it to him. He went through the pockets a second time and checked for hidden compartments, then concentrated as he manipulated the leather. "What's this thing in here? I feel something."

"Probably just the padding."

"No, this thing here. . . . Feels like it might be a wallet."

The cop found the rent in the lining and felt around inside, bringing out the library card. "Oh, whose name's on this? Let's see . . . 'Jack Lofton'."

"That's a friend of mine. I borrowed his card."

"Uh huh."

They put the name through the computer. The booking officer at the desk said, "Take off your shirt."

Lofton unbuttoned it, knowing what was coming.

"Come here, look at the screen. 'Born May 12, 1961—thirty-eight years old. Grim Reaper tattoo on left shoulder, barbed wire on right biceps, lightning bolts inside of forearms.'" He turned to Lofton with a hint of a smile. "How many people in Toronto do you think have a fucking Grim Reaper on their left shoulder?"

"Well, nobody, I would hope."

"You better pray your picture doesn't come up."

"Oh, fuck," Lofton said, "you got me."

"Well, well. And look at these outstanding warrants: 'Possession of a Prohibited Weapon', 'Failing to Appear'."

"You can add 'Theft Under' and 'Obstructing Justice'," the other cop said.

After he was charged and booked, he was ushered into the overnight holding area: a hallway lined with cells, each of which was monitored by a camera. Prisoners' shoes had to be left outside. It was almost two o'clock. Lying down on the metal cot, he pulled the blanket over himself and looked at the sink, the steel toilet, the ceiling.

3

Rowe decided to find some music. He got back on the subway and rode north to College, then caught a westbound streetcar to Spadina and disembarked by the Clarke Institute of Psychiatry. White bulbs rolled across the sign outside the Silver Dollar bar in the Waverley Hotel on the other side of the street.

He passed the pink and green neon palms of the El Mocambo as he drifted into the outskirts of Chinatown. Paved islands with shelters paralleled the streetcar tracks. The broad road was a long-time artery of the garment trade and home to various Asian restaurants and many disparate, shabby-looking businesses. There were window displays with dusty fedoras, wingtip shoes, X-rated videos. He paused by a striped pole to browse the designs inside the fly-specked glass of an apparent tattoo parlor/barber shop. Across the street and through the blocks around Baldwin, Kensington Market's shops and gamy stalls were closed until morning.

Blues chords could be heard over scattered applause as Rowe approached Grossman's Tavern. He opened the door and walked through the front area between some wooden tables and the bar, where an old hippie was nursing a draught and a Chinese woman was loading a tray with bottles. Two people were playing pool.

The adjoining room on the right was dimly lit and crowded. Rowe scanned the customers as he pulled out a rickety chair and sat down. There were primitive paintings of the building, and countless faded black and white photographs of regulars from decades past on the walls. The band was in the middle of a Sonny Boy Williamson cover.

Half an hour later he finished another drink and left while the musicians were on break. As Rowe stepped off the curb near the side of the building, he happened to notice a woman looking back his way while she walked up Cecil. It was just a passing glance, a wary gesture on a dark street, but he decided to follow her along the opposite sidewalk. When she emerged from the shadows into the light, he could see her long black hair and what appeared to be a pale trench coat. She looked back at him again.

The only sounds were their footsteps and the leaves rustling in the breeze. A white cat slunk beneath a car. Although Rowe kept a casual pace with his hands in his pockets, not wanting to alarm her, he was gradually overtaking her. Perhaps she was slowing down. He wondered if he should say something. Even in his unfettered state of mind he could see the unlikelihood of managing a conversation with her in such lonely and potentially dangerous circumstances, but there: she glanced back again. His pulse quickened. As they approached the first intersection almost parallel to one another, he caught her eye and said, "Excuse me. Would you like a cigarette?"

"Okay," she answered in a small voice.

They met in the centre of the road.

"My name's Derek," he said as he held out the pack.

She took one, smiling shyly. "I'm Sarah."

Up close he didn't find her very attractive, but she was unexpectedly young and there was something appealing in her suppliant stance and the tender way she was looking up at him. From her swarthy complexion he thought she might be Portuguese. "It's a nice night," Rowe said, lighting her cigarette, then his own.

"Yes." She barely inhaled.

"You're very pretty."

"Thank you."

He couldn't place her accent and wondered what to say next. It felt as if anything at all were possible. "May I give you a little kiss?"

She shrugged. "Um, okay."

He leaned over and put his hand on the side of her head, bringing his lips down to hers. She kissed him back. It was like a strange dream. "I'm certainly glad to meet you. Maybe we should go sit down so we can talk."

He took her by the hand and led her to a slight knoll partially concealed by a small tree just off the sidewalk. After they lowered themselves, he flicked his cigarette into the street and kissed her more seriously, slipping his hand inside her open coat and holding her by the waist. Then, moving upwards over her ribs, he palmed her small breast through her blouse and caressed it, feeling the outline and then the growing distinction of nipple unencumbered by bra.

Rowe looked into her dark eyes while he fumbled with the buttons and pulled open her shirt, trying to commit her tits to memory in case they vanished. As he caressed them she put her hand over his and nervously whispered, "People are there."

There was a couple walking up the next street. He leaned back on the grassy dirt and shifted his prick while she rearranged herself, and asked, "Would you like to come back to my place?"

"Okay."

She dropped her cigarette and stepped on it as they began walking. Rowe put his arm around her. He tried to piece together the apparent facts: her hair looked clean, the coat and slacks were all right, she didn't appear to be crazy, and her seeming naiveté didn't fit the standard hooker profile. Maybe she was some kind of angel. He asked, "Do you live around here?"

"On Beverley Street."

"Were you coming back from somewhere when I met you?"

"I was in the bar. Where you were."

"You were there too? I didn't see you."

At the corner of Huron and College they got into a cab. He took her hand in the back seat and said he was happy they'd met, but was surprised she wasn't worried about talking to strangers on dark streets.

"I was bored in my room. I didn't want to go back."

"You were looking for adventure."

"Yes."

"Do you have a boyfriend or anything?"

"Yes."

Rowe assumed that she'd misunderstood, and didn't pursue it. As he looked out the window it occurred to him that they weren't far from Beverley, and suggested that they go to her place instead. After telling the driver to take the next right, he asked her where she was from and was perplexed when she said India. It was getting so he couldn't tell where anyone was from anymore. The cabbie, glancing at them in the rearview mirror, could have been from India, Iran, or fucking who-knows-where himself.

"How long have you been here?"

"Three years," she said. "First year I was in Montreal."

"Is your family here or back home?"

"Home. I came here myself." She squeezed his hand and added, "I had a friend who came first."

The cab turned onto Dundas from McCall, a few blocks from 52 Division, passing the Henry Moore sculpture outside the Art Gallery of Ontario. As they drove down the next street she pointed out a three-storey building set back from the road behind an iron gate. After paying the driver, he followed her up a path past some bushes and a bicycle rack.

While she was unlocking the second door, Rowe looked through the window to the office, and scanned the mailboxes, bulletin board and list of tenants. They walked by a community room where people were watching TV, and climbed the stairs. On the third floor a girl coming out of a small kitchen said hello to her.

After they reached her room he went back down the corridor to the men's lavatory. It looked sterile for a rooming house. Flushing the urinal, he took a long drink of water from one of the taps to try to dilute the alcohol, and looked himself over in the mirror.

Her single bed was pushed against the wall. Above the opposite counter was a shelf with a few books and papers, then a row of cupboards where a photo of her with short hair was taped. "Nice picture," he said. "Where was it taken?"

"In Montreal. A place like this."

Her window overlooked Beverley. "If you don't mind my asking, how old are you?"

"Twenty-seven."

"You look younger." Rowe checked the foreign literature on her shelf and noticed a copy of what seemed to be *The Koran*. "I thought people in India were Hindus."

She giggled and pushed herself against him with her head down. "I lied."

"What do you mean?"

"I'm Afghan."

"Afghan?"

"I'm from Afghanistan."

"Why did you say you were from India?"

"It sounds better. It's a very big country next to us, and it's more . . . interesting."

He put his arm around her. "I don't know much about Afghanistan, but I'm sure you can be proud of it. And maybe you're too pale for an East Indian."

After helping her out of her clothes, he set her down on the edge of the bed and stood in front of her while he slowly unzipped his pants. She sat awkwardly with her thin arms crossed, then looked up at him with a shy smile as he touched her cheek. Rowe noticed her downy mustache as she put her fingers around the base of his erection and took most of it into her mouth.

Later, lying beside him, she fingered the greying hair on his chest and wanted to know if he had a girlfriend. Rowe said he'd been seeing someone, actually, and asked if he could smoke. She told him apologetically that it was against the rules. He lay back again, glancing at his watch as he put his arm around her. "So, what do you do for a living?"

"I'm getting welfare."

Her looks seemed to be waning as he took in her thick brows and the circles beneath her eyes, noticing that her face was quite gaunt. He still found her fragile body language disarming, however. "What kind of work have you been looking for?"

"Anything, I think. I had an interview at a restaurant, it was for a dishwasher, but the man started touching me in the kitchen and wanted me to . . . have sex with him. He had my address when I filled out the paper, and wanted to come here. I didn't know what to do, so I said yes. It happened quickly and I didn't have time to think about it, but I didn't want to do it."

"That doesn't sound too good."

"No. And I probably wouldn't get the job, either. It would be for nothing."

"Did he come over?"

"He came but I didn't answer the buzzer. He was pressing it for half an hour, and finally went away. I saw him leave out my window."

After a while she fell asleep. When he heard her light snoring, Rowe saw that it was after three. As he tried to ease himself from the bed, she woke up. "Where are you going?"

"I have to get up early."

She watched him pull on his pants. "When will I be seeing you?"

"Well . . ." Tucking in his shirt, he turned to reach for his coat. "Since I'm going out with someone and you said you had a boyfriend, it'd be a bit hard right now. But why don't I take your number?"

"I don't have a telephone."

"Oh." Rowe sat down beside her. "It'll get complicated if the woman I'm with hears other women phoning my place. If it's all right, why don't I come down and call on you sometime?"

"This week?"

"Soon."

"I might have to leave here. My welfare is stopping and I think I'm going to get evicted."

"How long have you been collecting it?"

"Here, two years. Maybe . . . maybe I'll look for you in the bar. Where we were tonight."

"Sure, if I don't see you before that."

Outside, Rowe lit a cigarette. While waiting for a streetcar, he decided that she was probably looking for a meal ticket now that her dough was getting cut off, and thought about her lying about being East Indian. Now, there was a whole different Third World hierarchy for you. Christ, if she'd lied about that, she'd probably lied about Afghanistan too. She was probably one of those Gypsies.

4

Jack Lofton was woken at six AM on Saturday, chained to the other prisoners, and driven to Old City Hall in a police van where he had to wait in a holding cell with fifteen other people until court began at nine-thirty. They were served packaged sandwiches and juice. He told his story to the public defender or "duty counsel," a young Chinese woman who advised him to request that his case be remanded until Monday, since it was evident that his friend wasn't going to show up. There was no point asking the judge for bail if there wasn't anyone to post a surety. He was then taken to a larger holding area in the basement to wait until two when everyone else was finished in court.

Lofton and the other prisoners who hadn't made bail were driven to the Don Jail. While waiting to be processed, they were fed Salisbury steak with vegetables and dessert on aluminum trays. During the strip search he had to lift his testicles, turn around, and spread his buttocks. His money, clothes, keys and other possessions were confiscated and taken to the property room. He was given a blanket, a blue jail jumpsuit, a pair of socks, a T-shirt, and a pack with a comb, toothbrush, toothpaste and small container of shampoo, then told to walk naked into another holding cell off the processing area to change.

Everyone there appeared to be a small-timer. He got into a conversation with somebody who'd been arrested for Fraud Over and Failing To Appear while passed out at his ex-wife's place after she called in on him. A little oriental punk who seemed to know the routine from the way he was talking to the guards and asking people for cigarettes and things went up to him and said, "Hey. Do you need a house?"

"Yeah."

"You want to bunk with me?"

"Uh . . . sure."

"Okay, come on. You stay with me."

Prisoners observed the new guys coming into the main lockup as they sat around reading newspapers or watching one of four TVs in a long narrow room lined on one side with two-man cells and a guard station. Opposite, there was a wall of bars, and beyond that a walkway; the windows behind were protected by metal mesh. Steel tables and stools were set up in the centre of the room, toilets and showers at the far end.

Everyone was locked up early for the night. A bunk bed in Lofton's new "house" stood against one wall of cinder blocks, across from a stainless steel table with connecting chairs that were bolted to the floor. At the back, a toilet and sink. Du produced some smokes and held up a match for his cellmate before he walked back to the lower bed, lighting his own. "So, what do you do? Why you here?"

"Oh, just some bullshit. . . ." Lofton leaned forward with his arm across his knee and took a contemplative drag. He wasn't sure why the kid had chosen him to bunk with, unless it was for protection. But that hardly seemed necessary, the way he'd been introducing him around like he was cock of the walk. Getting deodorant, scoring tobacco.

"I got picked up on probation violation," Du said. "It was *shit*—they picked me up when I was just walking home from school, man. Not fucking fair. There were all these things I couldn't do, like I couldn't leave the house except to go to school. All kinds of conditions. But I wasn't doing anything, they just grabbed me—"

"What were you in for originally?"

"Armed robbery."

"And they just gave you probation?"

"Time served too. Six months."

"Oh, so that's how come you know everybody."

"Yeah." Du drew on his cigarette. "It wasn't nothing. My friends and me, we went into a store and robbed it with a BB gun and a couple knives. You know," he added with a shrug, "just doing something."

"You're from Vietnam, right?"

"Yeah. Five years I been here."

Lofton flicked his ash on the floor. "They don't mind if you smoke?"

"Yeah, they don't fucking care. You clean up yourself in here."

"So your friends are out on probation, then."

"Yeah. The cops pick me up for *nothing*. Just walking home. Fuck." He shook his head disgustedly. "So, you. Really—what's the charges?"

Lofton smiled slightly and rubbed his jaw. "Just a comedy of errors, my friend. Last summer three cop cars showed up one night after I'd parked my bike behind my girlfriend's building. I didn't know what the fuck was going on when they pulled their guns on me. This other girl came out and said, 'Oh, no, it's not him, he's just visiting someone who lives here.' Apparently, there was a peeping Tom before I got there. You know, some guy looking in her window—"

"Ha!"

"Yeah, but they were already going through my saddle bag and found this nine-inch switchblade I got for my ex-wife, because she used to get off the bus late at night when there was this rapist around. I forgot I had it. So I was charged with Possession of a Prohibited Weapon, but never went to court about it. Yesterday I got caught shoplifting a knife from Canadian Tire. I almost never carry ID, not since I sold the bike, and figured there might be a warrant out on me so I gave the cops a phony name."

"Oh, man. You crazy like me."

"So there's an Obstructing Justice charge now too."

"Shit. How come you don't make bail?"

Lofton raised the cigarette to his mouth. Exhaling, he said, "My friend didn't show up. I don't know what the fuck happened, so I've got to phone him again and tell him it was remanded until Monday."

About an hour later, Lofton was on the top bunk reading a newspaper when a guard came by with cookies and hot chocolate.

"Our snack," Du said.

"What, they do this every night?"

"Yeah, yeah. Last night we got cake."

He came down the ladder. "This is like the fucking Hilton. They sure don't feed you fucking cookies and cake in the L.A. lockup."

"Los Angeles? You were there?"

Lofton sat on the stool and picked up a vanilla wafer. "That's where I grew up."

"Why you in jail?"

"Armed robbery," he said, "and attempted murder. I was found not guilty."

"Fuck, you wild guy."

Early the next morning after breakfast he had a shower. His wet hair was combed into a shaggy ducktail as he poured himself a cup of tea from one of two urns, and took a seat at the centre table to read a three-day-old section of newspaper. Later, he sat among the other prisoners watching television.

In the afternoon, Lofton was told he had a visitor. He and a number of others were escorted to a circular area where heavy telephones were affixed to a counter beneath a window of Plexiglas by steel cords. There were no chairs. When he saw Derek Rowe on the other side, he went over to the empty spot opposite him and picked up a receiver. "Well, you finally made it."

Rowe was dressed in a white dress shirt, but was unshaven and looked hung over. "I had to close the fucking store on Saturday to go down to the courthouse, but when I got there your name wasn't on the docket. They said you'd been transferred to another room, but I couldn't find you there either, and left."

"I forgot you had to work Saturdays. After seeing the judge, I had to go to a holding area."

"So what the hell's going on?"

Rowe listened to Lofton explain with one shoulder against the glass. "So it wasn't the liquor store, then. You said something about planning to steal a bottle."

"No. So I need you to be there for me in court on Monday."

"You need me to put up bail."

"You don't have to pay anything. Just sign, saying you're responsible."

"Like I said. It can't be more than a grand, because I'll have to prove what's in my bank account."

"Well I'm good for it, don't worry. The worst thing about this place is the boredom. The unmitigated fucking boredom of waiting in court, in the cells, getting processed into the Don, sitting around jail, being locked up after dinner. . . . I've got a nice cellmate though, this Vietnamese kid named Du. He can't do enough for me."

"Who fucks who?"

Lofton ignored him. "His lawyer sounded pretty incompetent by the sounds of it. There were so many stipulations to his probation that he was going to have to break it no matter what he did. Of course," he conceded with a wry smile, "nobody in this place ever did anything wrong. They're all innocent—just ask them."

"So, are you pleading guilty or what?"

"What can I say? They caught me red-handed. I'll just plead no contest. The duty counsel was this not-bad looking oriental, and it's funny, you know . . . she suddenly looked at me when I was talking to her, and said, 'What is someone like you doing here anyway?' I told her, 'I have no idea, believe me.'"

"So just why are you pulling this penny ante shit?"

Lofton brushed his hair back. "I don't know, *Mom*."

"You might have to do a few months in minimum security, like Mimico or Metro West. Are you getting a lawyer?"

"No, a duty counsel will be good enough."

"You sure?"

"I don't have any kind of defense worth paying for."

Rowe glanced around and asked, "What's the racial balance in the Don these days?"

"I don't know. A mix, I guess. I've seen more Mexicans in here than I've ever seen in my life."

"I didn't think Toronto had that many Mexicans. Are you referring to Hispanics in general?"

"No, I think Mexicans. I know Mexicans."

After Rowe left, Lofton went back to the main hall and played cards until everyone was locked up for the duration of the afternoon.

The next morning he saw Rowe sitting in court. When it was his turn, the prosecutor, or Queen's counsel, told the judge that since the defendant had no criminal record they were only asking for a small surety. The duty counsel said that Lofton had a friend who could provide up to a thousand dollars, so the judge granted bail for that amount.

It was a quarter after eleven. Before Lofton was taken to the larger holding area downstairs, he asked a court officer how long it might be before he got out, and was told about one-thirty, two o'clock. If you were polite to them, apparently they'd be polite to you.

There were about fifty in custody down there. He waited, watching the numbers thin as people made bail or were taken to other detention centres. The day dragged on. At three he asked a guard what the deal was, and was told that his guy must not have been able to provide the surety.

By four twenty-five, Lofton figured court was finished. There were only three others in the cell with him, and the Justice of the Peace had likely left for the day. He swore to himself as he looked through the window at people typing and walking around, knowing the phones in the Don would be cut off at five and he was fucked. Maybe he should call his ex-wife.

Hours later, he sat on a bench in the police van on his way back to jail. At nine-thirty, while waiting in a downstairs holding cell to be reprocessed into the general population, Lofton asked if there was a chance he could use a telephone and was told by a guard that he was going to be seeing the J.P. in about ten minutes.

He was taken upstairs to another cell, wondering what was going on. When he was led down a hallway, Lofton saw Rowe through a glass partition talking to someone, maybe a Justice of the Peace.

After he was released, they were both buzzed into the anteroom and stood by the benches waiting for the guard behind the window to release the second door. "Oh, man," he said, "I didn't know *what* the fuck was happening. All fucking day I've just been waiting around."

"You're welcome."

"You don't know what it's been like, having no idea what the fuck's going on hour after hour, all day long. I mean, I *saw* you in court, I knew you showed up."

He felt mildly exhilarated when they stepped out into the night air and walked down the ramp.

"I spent the whole day on this bullshit," Rowe said. "I didn't even get to see the guy until almost four o'clock, and when he looked at my bank book he said I hadn't had it updated in a couple of months, and gave me twenty minutes to get to a bank. I don't know why that made any difference; if I'd had it updated two days ago I could have still taken all the money out without using the book. I remembered there were Royal Bank machines at Queen and Yonge, but when I got there they were gone; it's a fucking Towers store now."

"I didn't know *where* you went. Do you have a cigarette?"

Rowe gave him one, and paused while he shielded his lighter for him. They started walking again. "I'd left the car in a garage because I figured I wouldn't have to go far, but when I finally found a machine it was too late and the courts were closed. So I had to come to the jail tonight to do it, and waited here for over an hour and a half."

"I wasn't even back from court yet. The bail shouldn't have been that high; the duty counsel should have gone for less."

When they got to the Firebird, Lofton waited for Rowe to unlock his door. As he settled into the front seat he put his cigarette in the ashtray, and pulled a red bandanna from his jacket pocket. "All right, let's go get a fucking drink."

5

After Marva Jones collected ten dollars for the table dance, she slipped into her bra, hooked the front clasp, and then stood with one hand on the edge of the table to aim a spike-heeled pump through the leg-hole of her thong. Picking up her small platform, she walked through the bar in an easy strut, showing off her long legs.

At twenty-nine she figured they were her best asset. Any weight she'd gained didn't show much on a toned, big-boned, five-eight black frame, though she could see the evidence in her driver's license picture. Her face was still striking for its cheekbones, but seemed broader than it had in the publicity glossies five years earlier.

She had sultry eyes and a smile she knew could raise the motherfucking dead. Her shoulder-length extensions complemented her boobs and the jut of that money-making booty. So what if size D tits made more money; they were the first to sag.

When Marva passed the washrooms and DJ booth, she stopped to talk to Vicky, a slender blonde with bad teeth leaning against the brass rail near the bar. It was then that she noticed the burly guy with the bandanna and spiky jacket she'd danced for the other night checking her out again from a table on the west side of the stage. Though she'd wondered from the earrings and tattoos if he was a biker, the older man he was with looked more like a cop, except maybe for those cowboy boots with the steel-capped toes.

"I see somebody," she said. "See you later."

"Yeah, later."

Marva picked up the platform and started walking. He raised his hand to catch her attention. She took a leisurely right between some tables and chairs, pausing briefly to brush off another customer until the next song. "Hi," she said, putting down her prop. "How are you tonight?"

"Good. How're you doing?"

"Okay. One of you want a dance?"

When Mr. Steel Toes suggested she perform for both of them, she gave him a smile and told him no, just one, so he said, "I guess Jack, then. He seems to have taken a shine to you."

"Yeah?" She sat between them and crossed her legs, glancing at the bearded one. "He looks kinda mad to me."

Her guy deflected attention by looking around the bar with a sneer as the smoke curled up from his cigarette. "They ought to turn on a few lights. You can hardly see a fucking thing in here."

"Like me, you mean?"

"No, you know what I mean. Everything."

"Well, you businessmen like to sit in the dark. You don't want to be seen in a place like this, right?"

He snorted. "Hardly."

"I'm Derek," the other one said. "I think you know our friend here."

"I'm Marva."

She made small talk while waiting for the next song to start, sniffing periodically to try to clear her sinuses. Although this Derek had a hardened sort of face with pockmark scars, the white shirt and short hair made him seem professional or at least more respectable. He also seemed easier-going.

She suspected from Jack's attitude that he was trying to impress her with his toughness. He was staring over her shoulder with a disgusted expression when he said, "Look at that guy there in the leather coat. Those aren't real handcuffs on the epaulets, just fag shit."

"What are you drinking?" Marva asked, reaching for his glass. "Can I have a sip?"

"Vodka-tonic. Go ahead."

The next song was "New Orleans is Sinking" by The Tragically Hip. She got up and stood on her platform. It was the second number for Candy-O on the low stage; she shed her bikini top, twirled on the pole, smudged the mirrors, and looked between her legs at the first row. Derek's attention was divided between the main act and a polite interest in Marva's limber movements beside him, apparently trying not to stare into someone else's ten dollars' worth. Once she was naked she noticed he was harder to distract.

With her hands on Jack's chair, she pressed her breasts within an inch of his stony face and slowly turned around, swinging her ass low and bending her knees to graze his lap with a light bounce, bounce, bounce, then up again, peeking at him between her thighs. She got down and pulled the next chair closer as she sank back on it, putting her legs on each of his armrests. Showing some pink. A black girl in a dark room had to work.

Jack raised his glass solemnly. "You're beautiful."

"Thanks."

Afterwards, as she was putting on her lingerie, Derek said, "When you finish tonight you should come out with us for a drink. If it's after hours we can hit a booze can in Chinatown."

"Well, I don't know about that." She gave them a non-committal smile as she walked away.

Marva was talking to a bald regular across the aisle, waiting for Randy to start the next set with another record, when Jack got up and walked past her in the direction of the washroom. She swivelled in her chair and said to the other guy, Derek, "Hey, what up with your friend? Is he always mad at the world?"

"He's a pussycat."

"Yeah? He looks kinda scary."

"You're the reason he wanted to come here tonight."

The opening of that ZZ Top song she couldn't remember the name of was on the sound system as the DJ introduced Ginger, who strolled out of the semi-darkness towards the stage. There was some applause from the back. Marva turned to her customer as she slowly got to her feet, and then stood on the platform in front of him.

Later, after her own final set, she was fixing to call it a night and go change when she paused to talk to Jane behind the bar. Anthony, the bouncer, asked if she wanted to go to his place for a drink.

"I thought you were coming out with us."

Marva turned around. That man Derek was standing behind her with kind of a smile, a thumb hooked in his pocket. She found herself blanking as she tried to concentrate.

"Um, yeah," she said, turning to Anthony. "They did ask me first."

He was kind of pissed off, but he was a dead end anyway. As she opened the door to the dressing room she could see it was probably stupid to go with them, but sometimes the Lord led you down mysterious paths. Or maybe it was the four Bacardi-Cokes.

She paused on the wet sidewalk outside the heavy wooden doors of Cheaters, and did up her jacket. "So, where are we going?"

"Somewhere there's a band," Jack said.

Derek unlocked some kind of muscle car at the meter with a pissed off Woody Woodpecker sticker in the back window. "Well, we haven't much time." After he got in and reached over to open the passenger side, Jack opened the door and climbed in after her. Marva noticed the full ashtray in the front, and the pair of furry dice hanging from the rearview mirror.

South on Yonge a band called The Meteors were advertised on a large sign by the parking lot of the St. Louis, a white bungalow made transparent by huge windows lit by neon beer insignia. It looked like a sports or country bar. "We don't have to line dance or anything, do we?"

"It's R 'n' B," Jack said.

As they pulled in crooked between two parallel white lines, she could see the group playing inside. Derek shifted into park and turned off the ignition. "All right, we'll still be able to get a drink."

They went in. Customers on the right side of the room were sitting at a long horseshoe-shaped bar. Marva followed the men around the corner to a table in the smoking section by the front window. It seemed to be after last call, so she took a seat while they went up to try to get served. After taking off her jacket, she checked herself in her compact and was annoyed to see that she hadn't covered her spots very well.

The singer, who looked Hispanic, was playing trumpet to what sounded like James Brown. She never got into that funky brass shit. Some of the older white people dancing looked like they could have been cowboys if they had the hats.

Jack set a rum and Coke down in front of her as he took the next chair. Derek sat across from them and said, "The bartender knows us.

"So, you're regulars."

"The guy's worked at a lot of bars around town," Jack said. "Before this he was at a place called Flick's." He turned to Derek. "You remember that place down the alley, north of Eglinton?"

"Now it's got the pool tables."

Jack offered Marva a cigarette but she declined. Leaning forward to be heard over the music, Derek asked her if she played pool.

"Sometimes, but I'm not that great."

"You should play with us sometime. We're not that great either."

Jack scowled. "Speak for yourself, homeboy."

"*Home*boy? Damn," she declared, "you two gangstas?"

"I just bailed him from jail for pushing his grandmother down the stairs."

Jack almost smiled. "Right."

Marva laughed. "Were you really in jail?"

He glanced at his friend with an exaggerated frown and waved it off. "It was just a misunderstanding. I'll tell you about it another time."

Marva looked around the room. There were a lot of things on the walls about sports and chicken wings, and a big red pepper hanging from the ceiling on the other side of the dance floor by the nonsmoking section. She wondered if any of the other girls from work came here.

"Whereabouts do you live?" Derek asked.

"About ten minutes from downtown."

"How long have you been dancing?"

"About a year," she answered, gazing past him to the band.

"You're good," Jack said.

"Thanks."

He downed the rest of his drink and went to the bar. When he came back he put another rum and Coke in front of her, and sat down with what was presumably a second vodka-tonic. "You drink too slow."

"You trying to get me drunk?"

Five minutes later, Derek finished his beer and said he had to work in the morning, which didn't make much sense after the trouble he'd gone through to get them there. Maybe the invitation had been a setup for Jack. She wasn't sure how she felt about it, but didn't think she could suddenly leave, not with a new drink sitting there.

After he was gone she said, "Your friend's really been watching out for you, hasn't he?"

"What do you mean?"

"Inviting me to go out after work, then getting us to the bar and leaving us alone. . . . When you went to the washroom before, he was talking you up and telling me what a nice guy you were."

Jack smiled slightly. "Yeah, well, he's kind of a mother hen sometimes."

Marva squeezed the lime into her drink, then dropped it in and twirled the ice cubes with her swizzle stick. "What did he really bail you out for?" She put the pink plastic sword in the ashtray, and took a sip.

"Well . . . basically, this woman was getting hassled by a guy, and I got into it with him and ended up getting charged with assault."

"You came to her rescue and had to go to jail?"

"Well, I sent him to the hospital and—I have to get a lawyer. I'm not sure what the legalities are just yet. He wasn't beating her up, but she was obviously scared and trying to get away from him, so I guess my defense would be that I thought she was in danger. I don't know if that'll hold up in court since I hit him first."

"Well, cops bust or shoot people all the time, and then ask questions. What'd you do to him?"

"Oh, he had a broken nose and lost a couple of teeth."

"So you're, like, a hero."

Jack's expression might have been suspicious. "No, sometimes I just help the less fortunate." He studied the band and then turned back at her. "The other day I got off the subway at Yonge and Bloor, and there was a Coke can on the platform which this student-looking guy accidentally kicked into the leg of this weird, reprobate type, who exploded into a rage. He was shoving the guy and screaming, 'What the fuck?!' or some shit like that, and the other guy was saying, 'I'm sorry! I'm sorry!' The system was really crowded, and all these people were ambling by pretending not to notice.

"I felt sorry for the student so I intervened and said, 'Hey, man, he's said he's sorry about fifty times. What's the problem?' Now the fucker was in my face. He shouts, 'You wanna box?'

Fists clenched but not raised. I put myself into the 'ready stance,' as I was taught in martial arts, feet planted shoulder-length apart, arms loose. I said, 'Do *you?*' Just then a couple of uniformed TTC guys happened to come down the stairs, and the guy took off, yelling, 'Fuck all you faggots!' He was obviously wasted on crack or something. A minor incident, but things like that get the adrenaline pumping."

Before she could respond, he continued. "And with animals especially—I fucking *hate* it when anybody abuses them. A couple of months ago, right, I was walking along St. Clair, and just before Yonge Street, outside the Scotiabank, there was this dog tied up to a parking meter—right out in the direct sunlight. It was really hot. He was panting fit to beat Jesus, and wandering around as much as he could, and whimpering. I went into the bank and pointed out the window at the dog and asked the lady at the service desk, 'Do you know who the owner is?' She was very nice, and said, 'Well, I'm not sure, but I think he's in the bank somewhere.' I said, 'Okay, well, I'm going across the street for a minute, and if he's still out there when I get back I'm calling the police.' Just then this guy comes trotting past us from the teller counter, and the service lady asked him, 'Is that your dog out there?' He said, 'Yeah,' and I said, 'That dog is really suffering, man.' He wouldn't look at me, and he ran out and untied the dog and went on his way at a distinctly brisk pace. Sometimes I forget how intimidating I can look. I've heard it said that I look like a Hells Angel whose Harley is in the shop. Anyway, that was my good deed for the day."

Now that all the lights were on, Marva tried to concentrate. Even if she wasn't drunk, alcohol always fucked with her thinking. He'd taken off his leather jacket and was wearing a preppy type of striped shirt with the sleeves pushed up beyond the zigzag tattoos, and was barrel-chested but not exactly fat, not yet, not for another few years maybe. Also, he smoked American cigarettes.

"What sign are you?" she asked.

"Capricorn."

"I'm Gemini. I don't know astrology that well, but my girlfriend's into it so I'll have to ask her what Capricorns are like one of these days. She's going through a lot of shit right now. Children's Aid took her kids away, and she's trying to get them back."

Jack turned his head to exhale. "How come?"

"I don't really know. I think her ex-boyfriend phoned them and lied that she took drugs and that they weren't getting fed, and stuff like that. I don't know exactly. He was kind of fucked up over her and wouldn't leave her alone."

"Are you two good friends?"

"We're all right. I used to know her from where I grew up, so we still get together and stuff."

"Where'd you grow up?"

"Jane and Finch."

"Tough area."

"Yeah, I had to get out. People live really badly sometimes. They have no respect, and write on walls and vandalize everything. It's dis*gusting*. I still have friends who live up there, and my mother too, because that's where she goes to church and knows everybody." Marva raised her glass. "Do you ever go?"

"Church? No."

"Never?"

"Not since I was a kid." He seemed to be looking at her funny. "Why, do you?"

"Sometimes."

"What religion?"

She felt self-conscious. "Well, it's a friend's church, I don't know what religion. It's very spiritual. Gospel music where people get more involved, not where you just pray or listen to a sermon. It's good to put on your best clothes . . ." She trailed off in case she sounded stupid. The musicians were packing up their instruments, and people were leaving. "Do you have any brothers or sisters?"

"I have a half-sister in Texas," he said, with a pull on his drink. "My parents split up when I was a kid, and I grew up in California. What about you?"

"I've got two brothers and a sister. Well, half-brothers and a half-sister. Everyone has a different father. The other fathers are in Jamaica; mine's in Brooklyn."

"Do you see him much?"

"No, he never writes or anything. I went to visit him when I was fourteen, and he never even came to get me at the airport. I had to find my own way to his place."

"Don't take this personally, but your father sounds like an asshole."

Marva sipped her rum and Coke. "Well, I guess he's got a new life. He didn't really know who I was or anything since he left when I was little. I wrote a couple of times after that, but then I stopped. My mother doesn't talk to him, so I don't know if he's still there, or even if he's alive."

"Wasn't he paying child support?"

"No, nothing."

When the staff was clearing out the remaining customers, she drank off her cocktail and stood up without knowing what was supposed to happen next. He didn't seem to have a clue either.

6

Lofton was waiting by the streetcar stop with her outside the subway at Queen when she suddenly hailed a taxi. He wasn't sure if she was bailing on him until she moved over to make room, and he climbed in beside her. Her assertion that she lived ten minutes from downtown was more than wishful thinking, it was a downright lie unless she meant by helicopter.

Her basement apartment was in a rundown Victorian manor in Parkdale near Sunnyside Beach. He went down the stairs with her at the side of the house, waited while she unlocked the door, and then looked for her refrigerator. As soon as he had a beer in his hand, he embraced her and they kissed against the sink.

Later, during sex, her expression grew disturbingly remote. When he leaned in on one elbow to kiss her, she turned her head away, her face a mask of savage illogic after the passion he'd aroused while eating her. "I wish we weren't doing this," she said.

So that's how it was. But she was wet and her nipples were still stiff. Despite the alcohol, Lofton was tense and insufficiently confident of his hard-on in the prophylactic after the booze to indulge this twist in her mood; he tried to focus on the act itself, how far along he'd come, the geometry of her spread legs and the grip of her pussy as he held her, giving her a few thrusts he hoped she'd feel tomorrow. He stroked her firm breast and slid a hand down her back, turning her slightly to grip a cheek and insert a fingertip into her tight asshole.

His ejaculation partially eclipsed the insult and hinted at a new phase in his life, post-divorce, with or without this stripper. He lay beside her and tried to relish his flawed triumph, wondering if he should get up and leave or give her a chance to explain herself. He wiped away some sweat as he straightened his bandanna, then reached over the side of her bed for his beer. He was still wearing his socks. "So, what'd you mean—you 'wish we weren't doing this'?"

She looked at him without emotion. "I meant so soon, the first night."

"Didn't you feel all right?"

"Things never work out if you go to bed with someone right away."

Lofton relaxed but wasn't entirely convinced. He offered her a drink. "Listen, that's the strangest fucking thing I've *ever* had anyone say in the middle of sex. You don't say that kind of shit to someone when they're fucking you. That's a goddamn mood killer."

Marva didn't look contrite. In fact, her face was maddeningly detached. Swallowing, she passed the bottle back. "Sorry, but I just have to say what I think. Whenever I have sex with somebody the first night, it always goes wrong. I should probably tell you, my relationships don't usually last very long."

There was a brief silence. "What happened with your last boyfriend?"

"I was engaged but he said he thought we should take some time apart. What do you think of something like that— 'We should take some time apart'?"

"How long ago?"

"A month."

Lofton put his bottle on the dresser beside him. His gut sagged as he turned and tugged the reservoir tip of his condom, and slowly began to roll it off. "How long did you know him before you got engaged?"

"A month."

"No, I mean, how long *before* you got engaged?"

"A month."

He leaned over and put the rubber on her throw rug. "You only knew him a month and you wanted to get married?"

"Yeah, you know, you look for Mr. Right. . . . But he told me to stop being stupid when I was asking him about us, trying to get some kind of idea about what he was thinking. I guess I wasn't feeling too sure about things. I wanted some, you know . . ."

"Reassurance."

"Yeah, but he said I was being stupid."

"And he hasn't called since."

"He phoned a few days ago and wanted to know if I wanted to see a movie," she said, twisting one of her braids. "He knows I'd rather talk because we've got things to say, but he wanted to see a movie. I told him I'd call him back because he woke me up, and when I did, he wasn't home. I know he went to see it without me. We've argued about that before—him not waiting to see if I'm going to go or not. He left a message after that but I didn't call back."

"White or black guy?"

"White. I won't go out with black guys anymore; they're too much trouble. They act too ignorant and full of themselves."

When she got up to go to the washroom, Lofton pulled aside the sheet nailed across her doorway and left the tiny bedroom, or alcove, or whatever it was, and lumbered out to the living room. A couple of well-worn chairs faced a TV, VCR, DVD and CD player. Above the sofa her basement window offered a view of the driveway at asphalt level. A spray-painted garbage can was visible between the yellow curtains. As he pulled his cigarettes from his jacket he noticed an unlikely law book on a shelf of DVDs and old video cassettes, and looked at some framed photos on the scratched coffee table of girlfriends, a teenaged Marva with some guys, maybe a tough-looking boyfriend or half-brother, and an older woman who was probably her mother. He flicked his silver lighter aflame, inhaled, and studied a professional-looking studio shot of her a few pounds lighter in a tank top and vinyl hot pants.

Lofton went into the kitchen for another beer. Before drawing back the sheet to reenter her bedroom space, he noticed a closed door beside what looked like a closet. "Is this a bachelor or a one-bedroom apartment?" he asked, lying back down beside her.

"A one-bedroom, not including this."

"Why don't you sleep in the real room?"

"I rent that out."

"What do you mean? There's somebody *in* there?"

"No, he's out. He works at night."

"You're saying you live with a guy?"

"He's just a roommate. I put an ad in the paper after this girl who was living here moved out, that's all."

She closed her eyes as she turned her head on the pillow. Lofton drank from his bottle, mulling her situation, when he became aware of something. "What's that stink?"

Marva laughed. "I had to fart."

He leaned back on his elbow. "You're kidding.*"

"Well, what would you do? It's just natural. You can't hold it in—you'll hurt yourself. I have to do another one, too."

"Hang your fucking ass off the bed."

She laughed as he pushed her hip with his knee, edging her from the mattress, when the telephone rang. They glanced at one another. He checked his watch while Marva leaned over to the nightstand and lifted the receiver. "Hello? Oh . . . hi. It's kinda late, you know." Her eyes became glazed. "No. No, I haven't seen it. . . ."

Lofton drew on his cigarette and tapped the ashes down the neck of an empty bottle. A poster of Bruce Lee in a martial arts stance was tacked up near the draped sheet. He looked around at the amount of stuff crammed into the small space: a rack of dresses, shoes, hats on hooks. There were various brushes, bottles of perfume, and unfamiliar afro-type cosmetics and hair products on her dresser.

When she got off the phone she shook her head. "I don't believe that guy."

"Who was it?"

"Oh, this guy who used to live here, an ex-boyfriend. Can I have some of that?" Marva reached for his beer. Swallowing as she passed it back, she said, "He wanted to know if he left his health card here."

"At three in the fucking morning?"

"Well, he knows I work late."

"When did he move out?"

"About three months ago."

"Weird time to phone."

Marva yawned. "I never saw a guy with a ring in his nipple before. For a big guy with tattoos, you don't have very much hair on your body."

He looked down at himself.

"Me, I'm hairy," she said, running her fingers along her forearm. "I don't know what's in my background; it's all mixed up from the West Indies." She lay back and studied him. "So, what do you do for a job?"

Lofton took a drag as he considered his words. Exhaling, he said, "Security work, consulting in private investigation—"

"You're a private eye?"

"Not now, but I was in L.A."

She looked skeptical. "So you mean you were a real private eye, like in *Chinatown*?"

"Yeah."

"How'd you get started in that?"

"I took an eighteen month program that cost six thousand dollars at the best detective academy in the States, and opened my own office." Lofton propped up a pillow. He was kind of pumped, and felt like talking. "I didn't join an agency because I didn't want to work with . . . One of the advantages of being

a private investigator, why it's such a popular fictional character, is because while they work in law enforcement, they're
seen as independent. I figured if I was going to work for an
agency I might as well join the police department. I also knew
I'd be doing a lot of insurance fraud, shit like that. It's bread and
butter work, but I didn't want to do that—taking pictures of
some poor bastard on compensation who's out roofing his
house. I preferred to work on the other side of the fence,
where a guy's fighting a compensation hearing, you know, and
establishing evidence to prove that he's really incapacitated." As
the words were leaving his mouth, he realized the improvisa-
tion didn't make much sense. "You see what I'm saying?"

"What other stuff? Cheating wives?"

"That's spousal activity," Lofton said, passing her the beer.
"There are some detective agencies that only do that, and they
advertise a flat rate. Workplace fraud is a big thing. People
stealing merchandise. And showing services—that's where, say
you walk into a muffler shop and the guy behind the counter
says, 'Okay, well, you need five hundred dollars' worth of work,
but I'll tell you what. Rather than having it done here, come
back to my place. I'll fix your car in my garage and charge you
two hundred bucks.' I'd be hired to investigate that, where the
staff is taking business away from the owner.

"Missing persons was another major one. People looking
for lost loves, missing children, things like that. Private investigation's a huge industry because police don't have the man-
power or man hours to investigate what they don't consider
top priority cases."

"So, why don't you open your own place up here?"

"I came up here for different reasons. I looked into it and
knew I'd need a lot of money to get back into the business. In
order to get licensed for Ontario I'd have to take various legal
courses, which I had no problem with, because the industry
isn't well served by people misrepresenting . . . You hear stories, like a guy hires somebody to find out who's fucking his

wife, and the detective ends up fucking the wife too. I have no problems with licensing procedures, because like I say, it doesn't help the industry to have these rogue people out there. I want to see them licensed.

"I figured my license would have cost about twenty-five hundred dollars in legal courses, because you have to know the PI and Ontario court systems, and stuff like that. That's why if you're licensed in California, you can't work as a PI in Hawaii, right? It's just like a lawyer. You have to pass the Bar in New York, Connecticut. . . . You're licensed for just one state, and in Ontario it's the same thing. I think the act is called the Investigators and Security Guards Act; it went into effect in maybe seventy-five. A lot of times you work with the police. What the police consider a routine investigation is not routine to a man whose daughter or wife has gone missing. Information is worth a lot. I used to think to myself, 'I'm the last lifeline for this guy. He's been fucked by the police, he's been fucked by attorneys, he's been fucked by the insurance companies. He comes to me, and I tell him what he wants to know.'"

Marva yawned and then seemed to refocus. "You said you did 'consulting' now?"

His ash dropped onto the sheet as he turned to reach for the empty bottle. Brushing it off, he said, "I'm not licensed up here but I do the odd freelance job as a security consultant. I still know what I'm doing, and I'm good at it too. I've done some missing persons, landlord-tenant stuff . . .

"A few years ago there was a shooting outside this West Indian nightclub, and the cops had a suspect but no witnesses. This guy's attorney called my old attorney, and he recommended me, so he called and asked me to look around, ask some questions, see if I could find any witnesses. I couldn't, but it's a long story. Based on my testimony the police dropped the charges—" The telephone suddenly rang again. "You're very popular, aren't you?"

"I don't believe this." Marva picked it up. "Hello?"

He watched her blank out again while she listened and answered yes, no. He dropped the butt into the bottle. Maybe she was hooking on the side. If the conversation was anything other than business it was remarkably toneless and one-sided. He scratched his scrotum and went to take another drink, but caught himself.

When she got off, she said, "It was Tyrone again. I don't know what he wants. Just this bullshit about a health card, then he's talking about nothing."

"Obviously he wants to get back together with you."

She lay on her side and propped her head up with her hand. "I don't think so. I think he's smoking crack. When he was living here he wasn't working or anything, right? But he'd go out with his friends all the time and wouldn't help with anything. I got fed up because it looked like he was just using me for a place to stay, and I told him to move out.

"He went back up to Jane and Finch, and was living at a friend of mine's place. When I'd phone he'd never pass on messages. I was up there at a party one night, and he was making a phone call in the bedroom where I was putting my coat, and I just, like, tapped him on the leg—just kidding with him, and I said, 'How come you don't ever pass on my messages to Lindsay?' And he jumped up and started punching me in the *head*."

"I don't like assholes who hit women."

"Yeah, I was, like, totally blown away. I could not believe it. So I started hitting him back, and the room got totally wrecked. I called the police but they wouldn't charge him because he told them I assaulted him first, and they said it was his word against mine. But I just tapped him like this" —she reached over and poked Lofton on the leg— "I wasn't even mad, I was just fooling. But the police wouldn't take my word for it and charge him even though he had a criminal record already."

"For what?"

"I forget. Assault with a deadly weapon, possession of a gun—I can't remember."

"Think."

She smiled tiredly as she swung her legs over the side of the bed and sat up. "I don't want to. Thinking hurts my head."

Lofton lay there while she went to the washroom. He heard the toilet flush across the hall. When she pushed the sheet aside and climbed back beside him, she asked, "So what's the story with your friend tonight? Where do you know him from?"

"Derek? I met him when I used to work security at a bar."

She pulled the blankets up. "What does he do?"

"He manages stores."

"What kind of stores?"

"Well, I remember there was a sports supply place, then a porn joint, and now he runs this little business bookstore." Lofton finished the beer and put it on the dresser. "That reminds me—I noticed a big book out there on one of your shelves, something about Canadian law. What the hell's that for?"

"I wanted to read about how the cops can shoot some-body without asking questions first."

"Did someone you know get shot?"

They were interrupted by the phone.

"Jesus *fuck*. Is it that dick again?"

"Probably." She gave him an odd smile. "Hey, why don't you pick it up?"

He hesitated, and then leaned over to take the receiver from her. "Yeah?"

There was a silence. Then a deep voice: "Who's this?"

"Never mind that. Who the fuck is *this*?"

The line went dead.

Within seconds it rang a fourth time.

"What's your name, fool?"

"Don't worry about it," Lofton said. "And don't fucking call here anymore."

"I be cuttin' your balls off, mother*fucker.*"

"You haven't got a big enough knife, Leroy." He leaned across her to hang up, but couldn't reach. She took the receiver from him and put it back. "Okay, now take it off the hook and leave it off. Yeah, that's right." He sighed and leaned back. "All right, you got anything serious to drink around here?"

7

The bookstore that Derek Rowe managed occupied the main floor of a converted nineteenth century house on a downtown side street. His employer was a CFA who supplied the actuarial and accounting market, stocked texts for local colleges, and ran an international mail order business. When he'd been checking references it seemed likely that he hadn't realized that Rowe's previous employer, City Books, dealt with pornography and coin-operated peep show booths.

The manager who'd preceded him had embezzled money, so the owner signed all cheques himself which Rowe prepared weekly to cover payroll, utilities, couriers and publishers. A freelance bookkeeper did the monthly bank reconciliations. Between sales, overseeing stock and the part-time clerk who handled shipping, Rowe was skimming from the till by telling customers the printer was down during cash transactions, and providing receipts from the calculator. He then edited the computer's inventory. Even with this covered he tried not to exceed reasonable shoplifting losses, so it didn't amount to much.

Rowe needed to move in a new direction. Robbing bank tellers on his own had given him a charge but wasn't very profitable when factoring in the risk, and he found himself occasionally thinking about maxing out his credit cards in Tahiti and declaring bankruptcy, or bringing Jack Lofton into a more professional heist.

Despite claims of PI work and political connections, Lofton hadn't held a real job in years and had got by at one time by pimping out his own wife. Although he claimed to be getting unemployment insurance while doing freelance security and consulting, that would have lasted twelve months at best. If anything, he was on welfare. And now there were the shoplifting, weapons, failing to appear, and obstructing justice charges. Having a loose cannon for a partner would probably have its drawbacks.

Sitting behind the counter, he watched a familiar loiterer in the art school section where the most expensive books were located. In a store where there wasn't anything interesting to read, people were generally there to pick up course material, not browse.

Over six feet tall, mid-forties, matted hair, dirty clothes. He never bought anything, and was crouching behind the edge of the wall looking at an expensive text where visibility was limited, even with the convex mirror. Track lighting illuminated a rectangular space further narrowed by bookcases. Rowe tried to monitor him through a gap in a computer book stand on the counter, but when he looked again the man was withdrawing a hand from the inside of his army coat.

Any shoplifting cut in on his margin for theft. Rowe got up from his chair and walked around the counter. "Excuse me. Did you just steal a book?"

The guy looked at him, startled. "No."

"Open your coat."

He stood up and pulled it wide apart. While there might have been a hidden compartment, nothing was visible. Rowe reluctantly apologized but wasn't sorry to see him leave.

He sat down again beneath an antique shade. The building had been around a long time. Crooked stained glass above the front window had apparently shifted during an earthquake eighty years earlier, and an old man once wandered in to tell him that he'd met his wife in 1952 in the finance section, which had then been someone's living room.

Robert O'Hara, the clerk, was working in the back. He had been a clean-cut student at one of the schools they supplied when the owner had hired him, but despite his politeness and interest in the stock market, Rowe had suspected from the chiseled face and predatory eyes that he spent more time working out than studying.

O'Hara had since dropped out of college, pierced his ears, grown his hair to his shoulders (which he wore at work in a ponytail,) and was in the process of becoming elaborately tattooed. So far he'd had both arms and half his back covered in dragons, flames, gargoyles, swords and other images of a gothic nature. On his own time he wore a ring in his nose. Apparently he was tens of thousands of dollars in debt for courses that had gone nowhere, and was now dealing coke. Rowe, who was now going to bars with him, knew he was fucked-up but thought him basically trustworthy, and had been considering asking him onboard for a robbery.

O'Hara used an alias at a second part-time job in a shady telemarketing company which sold office supplies to businesses at four or five times the market rate. Although it wasn't clear to Rowe if the practice was literally fraudulent or if the sales pitch was just misleading, the company had been exposed on an investigative TV program. Apparently there were an unlimited number of people in purchasing out there not paying attention. Those that did were unable to trace their original sales contacts. To hear O'Hara explain it, many departments near their year-end were willing to pay inflated prices so that their budgets wouldn't be cut, and he made a killing in commissions.

Rowe went into the back room, where the clerk was saving shipping records onto a computer. A ghetto blaster and old cassettes sat on a shelf over the garbage can and broom, squeegee, dustpan and mops. Beside the sink there was a filing cabinet containing the monthly cash register receipts, old phone orders and publishers' catalogues; next to it on the desk there were books, binders, papers, another calculator, and out-of-date trade show advertising. Ancient business cards, notes, garbage pickup and recycling schedules were tacked to the bulletin board.

"I came across an order here for a guy named Charles Hiscock," O'Hara said, looking up. His fierce blue eyes were expectant. "You know, 'His—cock'."

Rowe poured some coffee. "I once knew someone named Lowcock. I'd have changed my name to Highcock, at least."

"Or Monstercock."

Rowe added sugar and went to the refrigerator for milk. "Do anything interesting over the weekend?"

"I went to the Sanctuary and the Velvet Underground on Saturday, played some pool. . . ." He swivelled in his chair. "This guy I know came back with Betty and me to my place, and we, uh, had sex with her."

"You both had sex with your girlfriend?"

"Well, not at the same time. After I was resting, he kind of fucked her in the ass."

Rowe replaced the milk and stirred his coffee. He thought Betty was a dumb brat, if only because he knew she didn't like him. She worked as a dominatrix in a downtown dungeon and represented a part of O'Hara's life he only partially understood from allusions to leather fetish nights and S&M episodes with melting wax. Leaning against the sink with his arms folded, he said, "On another subject, I was just wondering something. Have you ever been arrested?"

O'Hara drew back with a mock scowl, and laughed. "Heavy question." He seemed unsure if Rowe was serious. "Well . . . I got into trouble a few times when I was younger, but nothing bad. Like, when I was sixteen I was walking home one night and saw this cat get run over. I stomped it a few times to put it out of its misery, but some people freaked out and called the police, and I got chased. They were prejudiced from the way I looked back then, because I had a blue

Mohawk and jack boots. I had to hide up on somebody's roof."

"You stomped on a cat?"

"Well, it was suffering. Another time I was wrestling around with a friend, and dialed 911 and yelled, 'Help, help, he's killing me!' Then the phone wouldn't hang up. This woman's voice kept going, 'Hello? Hello?' She was still there every time I picked it up. Five minutes later the cops were banging on the door and rushing into the room with their guns out. When I explained what happened, they threatened to arrest me."

Rowe put his mug on the edge of the filing cabinet. "Ever thought of pulling off a robbery?"

"You mean like a bank or something?"

"A store, a bank, an armoured truck . . ."

O'Hara pushed a strand of hair behind his ear, and said, "No, not really."

"Come on. You look like the kind of guy who's pulled a rip-off or two."

"Hey."

"I won't go into details," Rowe said, raising his coffee, "but I've done a few things along that line. I was just wondering if you had any sort of experience or interest in something like that yourself."

O'Hara frowned as he considered his answer. "Sometimes dope deals can be like that, but I've never gone into a store with a gun or anything. Why, do you want to rob a bank or something?"

"Oh, we're just talking."

"Wicked," he said, nodding. "I don't know if you're just joking or what, but let's just say I'm openminded."

"All right."

Five minutes later, O'Hara came out while Rowe was sorting invoices. "So that wasn't like a test of my honesty, was it? I mean, no money's gone missing around here or anything?"

"No, no."

"Who'd believe a conversation like that with the boss anyway?" He straightened a book on the shelf beside him. "Just in case it makes any difference, you remember I told you that my father used to be in the Satan's Choice, and he's in jail now?"

"Yeah."

"Well, he's got some rifles and guns stashed up at my mother's house."

"Really." Rowe leaned back and propped one foot on the edge of the desk. "I may just have to recommend you for a raise."

8

Aflying skeleton was painted on the outside of Sanctuary. There was a white wooden cross over the entrance, and a motorcycle propped on its kickstand inside the doorway. Under a low ceiling music pounded through a black space filled with a crowd in eyeliner, dog collars, leather and dark lipstick, many of them dancing in a dry ice mist pierced by flashing rays of light. The floor was bordered on the north side by netting and Frost fencing.

Robert O'Hara leaned over the pool table and shot the last ball into the side pocket.

"Bitching." Kim Ellison laid his cue across the felt and gave one of their opponents an effete handshake.

When the other man handed him a five, O'Hara asked, "You sure you don't need any blow?"

"Not unless you're going to lay some on me."

O'Hara picked up his black leather coat from a bench and strode past the men's washroom with Ellison in tow, pausing to glance at the dance floor before stopping at the bar under an old chandelier. Behind the bottles there were shelves of animal skulls he'd decided were those of a fox, raccoon, horse, and his favourite beast: the mighty wolf, with fangs intact. Above that a purple black light poster with a pentangle bore the words, "Devil's Right." Another, with Japanese writing, included the English translation: PAIN STATION. Barbed wire imagery was painted in white along the wall.

O'Hara tossed his hair over his shoulder as he reached into his pocket to pay the bartender for another round. "I think I'm going to go home after this," he said, leaning against the counter. "Betty's there waiting."

"Oh, stay out. There's nobody here I know."

"No, she's already going to be pissed off."

"Fuck, let's go to the Zoo Bar."

"I *can't*. I told you she's psycho right now. When she got to that party and saw me necking with Janet, she kicked me right in the fucking head, man. I don't need that tonight."

Even O'Hara had to admit that Kim was a bit of a freak with his dyed white hair and shaved-off eyebrows and superlong fingernails, standing there in his black turtleneck like some kind of skinny fey vampire or zombie. He was still almost a virgin since he never seemed to get any action, so his membership in that man-boy love society was basically a pose.

"I went to apply for a job as a security guard today," Ellison said, "and the guy just looked at me and laughed."

"You should've worn your Docs."

"I *did*."

O'Hara upended the bottle and wiped his mouth. "At the bookstore I had this strange conversation with Derek—you know, my boss—and he seemed to be hinting around that he was interested in me coming in on some kind of fucking armed robbery."

"Are you serious?"

"Yeah."

"He must have been messing with you."

"Well, one of his jobs was being the manager of the rifle department of some sporting goods place. He knows his way around guns, and he was trying to give me the impression he's got some kind of background in this shit."

Ellison put his arm on the bar. "What'd you tell him?"

"Nothing, yet. I still have to hear what the plan is."

"I don't know, Rob." He lilted emphatically, playing Auntie: "Sounds pretty w*ei*-rd."

"He's been around."

Ellison tried to peel the label off his beer. "How old is he?"

"Forty something."

He looked back at the dance floor. "Is he talking about a jewellery store or something?"

"I said I don't know yet."

"Because you know you need a fence to sell that kind of stuff."

"Fuck, listen to you," O'Hara said. "A 'fence'."

"I'm serious."

"He said something about a bank, or like an armoured car."

Ellison put a hand on his hip as he turned away. "You should find out exactly what he's done before."

They stood there, backs to the bar, drinking. Ahead, a disco ball revolved over the dance floor.

"I don't think bank robbers usually work in bookstores."

"Fuck, Kim, all I know is, he does seem to know about this shit." O'Hara shook his hair free. "The old man taught me the basics, but I think this guy was in a gun club and goes to a fucking range." As they walked alongside the bar to the left of some fencing, he looked for potential customers among the people standing around, sitting in booths or on benches. The decimals from the bass reverberated with his heart and thumped up his spine. Rounding the corner, they went into a dimly-lit sitting area which opened onto the dance floor, where he saw someone they knew coming from the coat check.

Rusty walked up and shook their hands. "Hey, degenerates, how're you doing?"

"Rob wants to leave," Ellison said.

O'Hara ignored him. "What are you up to?"

"Nothing. I was just over at the Black Bull. Anybody here?"

"Jake and Ariel, but they left."

"They went to the Gypsy." Ellison gazed at the dance floor with a bored expression, a hand on his hip and his cheeks sucked in.

When they moved closer to a light, O'Hara got a better look at Rusty's black eye. He was already a rainbow with the blue hair and red beard, not to mention the fucking plaid pants and the snake tattoo on his neck. Sometimes he even wore a kilt. "Beautiful shiner. How'd you get that?"

"Some asshole bouncer. Come to the bar so I can get a drink."

O'Hara commiserated as they walked together. "I got into a scrap last week. I didn't want to hit the guy but he hit me first, so . . ." He switched the bottle to his other hand and gave the air a few downward jabs.

After being served they sat on a black bench built along a divide in the centre of the floor, trying to talk above the noise. "So," Rusty asked, "how's the capitalism doing?"

O'Hara wondered if this was a criticism of his counts. "What?"

"You were telling me about your investments."

"I was?"

"At Chester's. You were wasted."

"Oh . . . yeah." He watched the pool table. "I've been playing the market. I might take some more courses and get my MBA."

Rusty laughed. "No offense or anything, but I don't see you with a briefcase."

"He was at the School of Business," Ellison said.

They listened to the music and watched people go by.

"You interested in any coke?" O'Hara asked.

"I'm not getting paid until Wednesday, but if you want to front me a line."

O'Hara looked around. "Come into the can in a few minutes. I'll try and get the last stall. Knock twice on the cubicle door, and go in when I come out. It'll be in some foil on top of the toilet paper thing."

After he left the Sanctuary, Robert O'Hara walked east along Queen towards Bathurst with his hands in his coat pockets, jaw clenched when he wasn't working the gum. He looked into the Gypsy Co-Op bar before continuing past a hair stylist and used books shop, glancing at a Doc Martin window display and then his face in the dusty glass of Ecstasy Perfumes. The church at the bottom of his street had been painted with graphics and turned into a crafts shop and restaurant.

He prepared himself for a hassle as he walked up Euclid. Even though he'd told her he had business to do, Betty was probably waiting for him with a goddamn whip or something unless she got tired of hanging around.

Some of the attached houses on the narrow street had modern refaced fronts, others traditional ornate touches. Numerous clotheslines hung in small front yards. A real estate sign in English and Chinese was planted in front of a property in a row of nearly identical brick homes. Being late September, the hedges were still leafy and a few flowers were still around.

In the next block, past Robinson, O'Hara thought he noticed someone standing just off the sidewalk around his place. He squinted but it was too dark. If somebody she knew was waiting for him, Betty probably would have invited him inside. Bitch did have some manners. Weird how she'd re-named herself after that bondage model from the '50s. Maybe he'd do another line when he got home if she wanted to fight instead of party, or even the other way around.

O'Hara reached the schoolyard and crossed the road, stopping short when someone stepped out from behind a tree in front of his house. A car door opened. As the first figure came into the light he saw it was the greasy dude he'd sold all the coke to a few weeks earlier, the one who'd implied that he had biker connections. They'd talked about his father and The Choice, and the Angels in Quebec fighting the Rock Machine.

"Vince, right?" O'Hara glanced over his shoulder at the other guy walking up behind him. "Did you knock on the door?"

"Yeah, your girlfriend said you'd be home any time. That was over an hour ago. This is Frank."

O'Hara turned. The other guy was bigger. "How's it going?"

"Listen, man," Vince said, "that coke you sold me was sub-par, and a lot of people are pissed right off. It was really fucking cut."

"Nobody else complained." He found himself getting boxed in.

"No, it was fucking bad. You've got to replace it, or we need the two thousand back."

"I'm not in the business anymore. I stopped dealing." He was trying to shoulder past them when Vince suddenly shot an arm out and grabbed him by the throat. One leg buckled, but he got a foothold and managed to grip the man's collar before a heavy fist caught him behind the ear.

Frank got around him as they were struggling, and cracked him on the head with what felt like a pipe before O'Hara was hit in the ribs. As he turned, going down, he caught a glancing blow near the eye. Vince punched him while the larger man put the boots to him. He yelled for help as he tried to fight back, before pulling up his legs and covering himself on the ground.

"Get my money, fucker!" Vince shouted at him.

Frank kicked him in the kidneys. "We'll be back."

Lying there, O'Hara half-heard them walking away. Then the sound of car doors slamming, a motor turning over. As he struggled to his knees, he was aware of blood on the pavement.

9

Jack Lofton, drinking a 946–ML bottle of Schlitz from a paper bag, caught a bus from the St. Clair station to a stop near Derek Rowe's apartment building. It was twilight as he crossed the intersection. After being buzzed in, he passed a shelf of discarded advertising under the mailboxes, then climbed the steps and opened a second door to the first floor hallway.

Although he wasn't drunk, not yet anyway, he found himself veering towards the wall. Straightening his course, he turned right at the corner and headed towards the staircase.

Rowe was drying his hair with a towel when he answered the door in his trousers and undershirt. There was a pair of ratty looking slippers on his feet. Lofton followed him inside and sat down on the sofa as Rowe went into the bathroom. Crossing his legs, he pulled his bag from the bottle and took a drink. Hank Williams or some other prehistoric country music was playing. "You going out?"

"Maybe." Rowe walked into his bedroom. "Why, you want to go somewhere for a drink?"

"No, I'm going to see Marva." Lofton put his beer on the coffee table and took off his jacket. He glanced at the magazines in the shelving unit to the right of the doorway, and thought about getting up to see if there was anything decent, but was too lazy.

Rowe was tucking in a navy blue turtleneck as he walked into the kitchen. When he came out, he had a beer in his hand. "So, how's that going?"

"All right. She might be a bit flaky, but she's got the bitchingest body—well, yeah, you've seen it, haven't you. I'm usually not that attracted to black women. I mean when I see them in skin magazines I don't usually pay that much attention because they're so dark you can't really see the details. Even if they're totally fucking naked you think maybe they should undress some more." Lofton took another drink. He wanted to talk her up but didn't feel like sounding sentimental if his doubts were valid. "At first I thought she was as dumb as a bag of hammers, but she's pretty fuckin' sharp, actually."

"Yeah?"

"You better get used to seeing her around."

"It sounds serious."

"Maybe. . . . She's got some fucked up friends, though." He reached over and slapped his jacket, feeling for his smokes. "This guy, this old boyfriend or something, was calling at four in the morning until I got on the phone and told him to fuck off. He's supposed to be some fucking gangster or something."

"That doesn't sound good."

"I don't expect he'll be back." Lofton took a drag and clicked his lighter shut. "Another friend of hers—I think she's a welfare mother or hooker or something—her kids were just taken away by Children's Aid. The fact is, is that she *knows* they're fucked up. She's even religious, for fuck's sake. We had sex and talked until the sun was coming up. It was nice."

"Good thing we invited her out, then." Rowe took a drink and pulled one slipper back on. "You know Robert? You've met him. Works with me in the store."

"Yeah."

"Apparently he got beaten up pretty bad. Wasn't at work for a couple of days."

"What happened?"

"His girlfriend phoned Tuesday night and said he got jumped by a couple of guys outside his place and had to go to the hospital, and wouldn't be in for a couple of days."

"Do we know why?"

Rowe smiled. "Listen to this. When I saw him today he told me some fucking story that didn't make any sense. He said that he and his girlfriend had a friend over for dinner, and when the friend was leaving later that night he asked Robert for twenty dollars that he said he owed him. The two of them were standing on the steps just outside the back door, right? He lives in a basement apartment.

"So Robert goes, 'What twenty dollars?' The guy says, 'The twenty I lent you two weeks ago.' So they disagree about this money, then the guy grabs him and drags him up these steps, and pulls out a lead pipe and starts whaling on him. Robert says he was in his pajamas and couldn't really fight back. Then this *other* guy comes out of the shadows, and he has a pipe too, and they're both beating the shit out of him."

Lofton had to urinate, and shifted his weight. "Why's he in his pajamas?"

"They were having an orgy for all I know. He and the girlfriend seem to get into some funny shit, so I didn't ask about that part. He said he managed to get back into the house, and collapsed on the floor covered in blood. She called the cops."

"Who was this other guy? How long was he out there?"

"Well, this is what I'm saying. None of it makes sense." Rowe drank some beer. "If the guy was going to ask Robert for the money, the other one would have to be waiting outside all night on the off chance that Robert wasn't going to pay off a lousy twenty. And this is someone they're friendly enough with to have over for dinner, or whatever—a guy who's brought a pipe with him, and who has another guy with another pipe outside, and who's going to wait patiently until it's time to go home before suddenly trying to beat his head in for twenty bucks."

"Yeah, that story's bullshit," Lofton said, getting up.

In the washroom he swayed a little at the toilet. Urine hit the floor. On a shelf in front of him there was a bottle of

Scope, sponges, Bayer Aspirin with stomach guard, disposable razors, Ajax, deodorant and a can of shaving cream. Someone had tied a lacy hair ribbon to the blinds cord. On the upper half of the walls, above the yellow tile, the paint was buckling.

After he flushed, he walked back into the living room. Over the grey sofa was an art poster he liked with a painting of a fighter being knocked out of the ring. As he made his way around the coffee table, he asked, "So, are the cops involved?"

"Robert said they were looking for both of them, but neither of them have a fixed address. I assume it's a drug thing. He seems to do a lot of coke, but I get the impression he doesn't want me to know how much."

"Gotta be." Lofton settled down again. "And now everybody on the street probably knows he's a rat."

"He said he was thinking of moving. He doesn't want to testify, either."

"Of course not."

Rowe had a pull on his bottle, and smiled a little as he crossed his legs. "Speaking of Robert, he's interested in coming in on a heist of some sort that I've been meaning to talk to you about as well. Have you ever considered robbing some place like a bank?"

Lofton snorted and reached for his beer. "Where's this coming from?"

"Something with a reasonable payoff that might take two or three guys. Robert apparently has access to some unregistered guns and a rifle. At least as far as he knows, nothing's traceable. They'd just be for show; we wouldn't want to complicate things."

"First of all, you never bring out a gun unless you're prepared to use it." Lofton drew on the cigarette. Rowe was obviously fucking around because he liked the sound of his own voice, the narcissist. He'd go along with the conversation long enough to put a dent in some of his booze. "And I don't really know Robert a whole lot, but he's not the sharpest fucking tool in the drawer, is he? Look, I wouldn't rob a bank—they're too guarded and exposed. Something like a trust company or a utility company would be better, where people go in to pay their bills. And I'd go out of town, some place like Oshawa or Whitby."

"Banks are all right," Rowe said. "I've done two of them here in the city."

Lofton looked at him. "All right, let me get this straight. You're saying you've robbed two fucking banks. Is that correct?"

"Yes. Give me a cigarette."

Lofton felt around for the pack. "And when was this?"

"One in March, one in May. I don't want to say where. I just used a note, and picked up twenty-eight hundred bucks and then thirty-five."

"Well, I know neither one of them was a Canada Trust," Lofton said. "They never get robbed because of the way they have all the cash in an enclosed area. You ask them for change for five bucks, and they've still got to go back to a cage."

"Right. The store has an account at a branch on Bloor. For some reason all the wall cameras behind the tellers were taken out during renovations, except for one. It's been like that for months."

"Well, they're watching you. Believe it. Every time there's a bank robbery, it's always a Royal, a Bank of Montreal, Scotiabank or a CIBC or something, because they don't have that setup—yet. And that's not much of a payoff for the risk you were taking. Anyway, you don't need more than one guy to do a bank if you want to stick to the note—"

"I realize that," Rowe said. "I want to empty all the cash drawers. I want to go in, get the customers on the floor, and get everything accessible."

"If you're going to go in strong, you'd need more than two guys then. And of course no safes, not with time-release locks." Lofton raised his big bottle as he thought it over, and watched Rowe rummaging through his tapes. "Don't put on any more of that hillbilly shit."

Rowe returned to his seat as some blues kicked in. "By the way, did I ever tell you I met Johnny Winter in New York?"

Lofton squinted. "I think I'd remember that. When was this supposed to have happened?"

"Nineteen-ninety. A girlfriend and I went to a bar called Manny's Car Wash to see a guy named Lazy Lester. On the way there, we had to get back out of a gypsy cab trying to charge a flat twenty bucks. Driver tried to tell me that it was a long way and that anyone would charge that much. Took a regular cab with a meter instead, and it was like six." Rowe smiled. "Fucking New York.

"Anyway, Lester, this older black guy, is taking pictures of all the babes in his audience with an instamatic hooked to his belt while his band was warming up the crowd. Oh, I should mention that the bar was packed, but we somehow lucked out with an empty table right in front of the stage.

"So I happened to turn around, and I'm amazed to see Winter sitting right behind me with a woman. I didn't say anything because I didn't want to come off like an idiot fan. Then Lazy Lester noticed him too and came over to talk to him. I saw him looking around and knew what he was thinking, so I said, 'Excuse me, are you looking for someone to take a picture of you and Johnny?' He said, 'Yeah,' so I borrowed his camera and took photos of them with their arms around each other. Of course, *my* camera was back in the fucking hotel room. Then I shook their hands. Winter headlined the first rock concert I ever went to. I think I was fifteen.

"So then Lazy Lester kicks his own guitarist off the stage and asks Johnny up, who just happens to have his guitar with him. So now Winter's playing with Lester's band about ten feet in front of me, and all I could think of was my camera back at the hotel."

"I guess you couldn't have asked Lester—"

"Fuck no." Rowe laughed. "There's no way he was going to make copies and send them to me. His name's Lazy Lester."

Lofton snorted. "No, I guess not."

"Anyway, what we were talking about. . . . In some banks in the States you've got to go through a metal detector at the front door now. If you set it off, the doors in front of you and behind you automatically lock so you're trapped. It's probably a good time for tellers to cooperate these days, what with those Jamaicans blowing that woman's head off. You know, with the shotgun in that restaurant." He shook his head. "Fucking morons couldn't understand the concept of a time-delay."

Lofton finished his beer. "With that stuff in the news, it might not be such a good time. Security will be beefed up everywhere."

"We just check the places out first, that's all. I'll have to get some more details about the guns from Robert if he isn't in Mexico by now."

Lofton wondered what Rowe had in the way of liquor. "It doesn't make much difference what kind of gun it is, if you're looking down the wrong end of it. You can get shot point blank with a thirty-eight and be okay if it goes through you without hitting a vital organ. With a twenty-two—because it's a small round—it could hit your rib and bounce up to your collarbone, then go somewhere else. Get shot in the shoulder, and it ends up taking out your liver. You got any scotch?"

"I still want to see what he has." Rowe sat back with his bottle.

"You got any scotch?"

"Are you in?"

Lofton still didn't believe he was serious. He knew, however, that Rowe was going to have to be humoured if anyone was going to get a real drink. "I don't know. What the hell, maybe."

10

A couple of weeks later when the forecast called for rain, Rowe phoned an ex-clerk who had a job flying hot air balloons, to see if he'd be free to cover the store.

He drove Jack Lofton and Robert O'Hara to Yorkdale Shopping Centre on the northwest side of town to locate another car, and found an unlocked Subaru 4–door in the parking lot. The others waited by the mall entrance with a satchel and knapsack while Rowe hot-wired it and drove around to pick them up.

On the westbound 401 there was conflict when Lofton produced a bottle of rye, as Rowe didn't want to draw attention with guns in the car or get fucked up when they needed their faculties. O'Hara leaned forward from the back seat for a taste. His scalp was stapled and his face had contusions of varying shades. A bandage covered a potential scar alongside his black eye where he'd refused stitches. Lofton passed the whiskey back and pulled out a pack of cigarettes as Rowe scanned the radio.

O'Hara handed the bottle to Rowe and suggested turning to The Edge, but he said he didn't want anything loud. After a swallow he passed it to Lofton and fiddled with the FM again, stopping at something mid-tempo.

Lofton rolled his window down. "I still think we should've gone outside the city and hit Oshawa Public Utilities or something like that. They're not watched like banks, and they're not trained like bank employees."

"We covered that. Lots of cheques, VISA statements, no cash."

"I told you—people bring in cash too."

"Derek, do you have an extra smoke?" O'Hara asked.

Rowe glanced in the rearview mirror. "I thought you were trying to quit."

"No point today."

"You should put your hair in a ponytail and hide it inside your collar," Rowe said, passing the deck back.

"You got a light?" He waited for some matches. "You know what we ought to do? We ought to rip off some dealers."

"Like you, you mean," Lofton said.

If there was a response, it wasn't audible over the rear speakers. O'Hara was looking out the window with a resolute expression. His granite face looked unpleasant in the grey light.

"I still don't know why you told me that shit about getting beaten up in your fucking pajamas," Rowe said, pushing in the dashboard lighter.

"I was messed up." O'Hara brushed his hair aside and put the cigarette in his mouth. Taking it back out, he said, "I didn't want the boss thinking I was some heavy doper or something."

Rowe took the rye from Lofton. After a drink, he passed it over his shoulder and picked up his cigarette from the ashtray. "You feel okay now?"

"My ribs are sore, but yeah."

"Did they get cracked?" Lofton asked.

"No, just bruised."

"Cracked ribs hurt like a motherfucker," he said. "I got into a fight with two guys last year who tried to roll me. Believe me, it doesn't happen often, but I got the worst of it. Doctors don't even bother taping you up anymore."

Rowe passed the lighter back. He noticed that Lofton seemed on edge as well. Tapping the wheel, he put on the indicator as he checked his blind spot to change lanes. They were already past Highway 400.

"I can't believe we're actually going to do this," O'Hara said, returning the lighter.

Rowe took a damp hand from the wheel to roam the dial. "You're an outlaw now."

"I've been an outlaw since the day I was born," Lofton remarked dryly as he looked out the window.

O'Hara pulled his hair into a ponytail. "Heavy, man. Born under a bad sign."

Rain began to fall as they approached Islington. The Labatts' brewery loomed near the next overpass. Rowe turned on the wipers and got into the collector lanes, then, checking the traffic around him, reached for the mickey. "We don't want to lose our edge," he said, tilting it for a quick swallow.

Lofton blew smoke towards the ceiling. "Splitting a mickey three ways? Fuck, don't get me drunk."

Rowe glanced in the rearview mirror as took the off ramp. He'd picked a branch of the Toronto Dominion for its uncongested escape route along the nearby 401, having familiarized himself with the locale one afternoon when customer traffic had been light. There had been no sign of a security guard.

They drove north past some low buildings and a Sears tower on the left, then an open tract of land where truck trailers were parked. There was a plaza on the right, and another to the west where Rexdale Boulevard branched off. After some trees and apartment buildings a mile or so north of the highway, they came to a long, wide swath of field with hydro transformers fading into the horizon on either side of the road.

"It's just up here on the left," Rowe said. "In that mall behind the gas station."

Lofton and O'Hara looked out the window. There was a Greek Orthodox church on the southwest corner. Opposite, to the rear of a Petro Canada gas station, a small plaza was built on an angle with access routes to both Islington and a side street. Rowe turned into the driveway and slowly drove by a bakery and BiWay, barber shop, market, pharmacy, dry-cleaners,

Scotiabank, convenience store, restaurant, Toronto Dominion and hair salon. "I picked a place with two banks for good luck," he said, heading towards the other exit.

"Now where are you going?" Lofton asked.

He turned left, then put on his signal at the lights. "We're going to regroup."

The rain was light but steady as they drove south. Rowe pulled into the lot of the strip mall north of Rexdale Boulevard, and wanted to know if anyone else needed to take a leak.

"Is that why we're here?" Lofton asked.

"I want to cover a few things first. I'll be back in a minute. If anybody's going inside for anything, you should go separately so there're fewer details for anyone to connect us to the bank."

"Christ." Lofton looked out the window.

Rowe stepped into the drizzle. As he walked up to Coffee Time, he wondered if he was over-analyzing it. Mathematically, the odds of fucking up were proportional to the number of people involved. Aside from potential errors multiplying, suspects had a tendency to roll over on one another later.

As Rowe stood at the counter, Lofton passed him on his way to the washroom. He'd obviously been drinking before they got together. Sometimes it was only apparent by the degree of difficulty in dealing with him.

Back in the Subaru, Rowe took a sip of coffee and offered some to the others, passing the cup back to O'Hara. "We'll have to get rid of the bottle so we don't leave anything behind with fingerprints, including the car."

Lofton took a final swig and pulled out his shirt, sighing as he wiped the bottle elaborately. "Do you know how little they actually *use* fingerprints in court—what the odds are of getting a good sample? That's mostly fiction. Fucking DNA's what you've got to worry about now." He paused before unlatching his satchel and taking out a pair of thin leather gloves. Putting them on, he wiped the mickey again and glanced around as he cracked the door, putting it on the ground. "Satisfied?"

"You're getting on my nerves."

"Let's just do it, homey."

Rowe looked in the back seat. "Okay, give me the Glock. Jack gets the Beretta. You remember how to load the Ruger?"

"Yeah." O'Hara rummaged in his knapsack and handed him the .40 caliber, then the 9MM to Lofton. He checked the writing on the boxes of ammunition before passing them over the seat. "How come you guys get the semi-automatics?"

Rowe finished loading shells into the clip, which he slapped into the butt of the light polymer frame. "That Ruger's fucking nice. You got a good thirty-eight special there. And it couldn't possibly be registered, because the barrel's too short for it to even be legal in this country."

"Plus, a revolver's more reliable," Lofton said. "Less jamming."

"Remember, I told you that none of the guns are registered," O'Hara said. "My father's prohibited from owning any."

Rowe laid the Glock in his lap and sipped his coffee. He looked in the rearview mirror. "You loaded?"

"Almost. There better not be a shootout, because this only takes five rounds."

"That's the idea. The guns are just to keep the peace. Make sure the safety's on. . . . All right, pass that bag over."

"But you still have be prepared to use it," Lofton said, "if necessary."

Rowe opened the door and poured the rest of the coffee out, then tossed the cup and lid under the car. He took the shopping bag by the handles and brought it into his lap, reaching inside and handing balaclavas to Lofton and O'Hara. He took one out for himself, then a pair of gloves. "Later, don't forget to wipe everything down that you might have touched in here, all right?"

"I couldn't really work the trigger with my other gloves, so I brought these," O'Hara said, holding up some turquoise latex.

Lofton glanced back and snorted, then turned to Rowe. "They're not going to be able to isolate our prints from millions of customers'."

"Our prints are on file, so don't fuck around." He glanced back at O'Hara. "Keep your hands in your pockets from the car to the bank." Checking the rearview mirror, he put the car in reverse, wishing he'd had more of that whiskey.

"You guys don't want to snort a line first, do you?" O'Hara asked.

Rowe hit the brakes.

11

He went over the plan again on their drive back up Islington. Robert was to stand on the inside of the door where he could keep an eye on the idling car and block any incoming customers from leaving.

"You sure you don't want him in the car so we can get the fuck out of there fast?" Lofton asked. "That's usually how it's done, you know."

"We need him inside so we can get through the tellers quicker. Robert, keep them on the floor with their heads down. And if anyone can fake an accent, do it." Rowe drove through the intersection and slowed down as they approached the plaza. "If we get them down as soon as we go in, they might not notice our eyes and just think Jamaicans or whatever."

"Jamaicans with turquoise gloves."

O'Hara pulled up the collar of his army coat as he tucked in his ponytail. "We'll be the fucking Dishwashing Bandits."

Rowe turned into the driveway and pulled into a space. "I'm going to leave it running in front of the bank. We walk up with the bags, guns in our pockets, and keep our heads down until we're going inside, because the first cameras are by the cash machines."

"You going to put on the blinkers?" O'Hara asked.

"What? Yeah." Rowe turned to Lofton. "And we just want twenties, fifties and hundreds."

"Obviously. So why the TD and not the Scotiabank?"

"I just had a better feeling about it."

He drove over and parked the wrong way by the curb, facing Islington, and flipped on the indicator. "And don't lock the fucking doors."

They walked up. Rowe stopped the others outside the front and looked through the glass for the positioning of the cameras. Turning his back as he went in, he pulled down his balaclava. Masked, O'Hara and Lofton followed. At the second set of doors Rowe rushed a woman coming out with his Glock drawn, and pushed her back inside, shouting, "Everybody on da fuckin' floor! Dis is a robbery! Everybody down! Face *down!*"

There were nine or ten customers in line. They turned, one of them in a half-crouch, confused, others standing frozen, a woman already going to her knees. Lofton waved his gun alongside him, and O'Hara got into position by the doors, ordering Rowe's woman to the floor in what might have been bad Cockney.

"Nobody hit the alarm!" Lofton shouted, aiming up and down the row of tellers with his left hand gripping his right wrist. A middle-aged man standing at the counter hadn't moved, so he stepped over and hit him in the head with the gun barrel. There was a scream as the customer's knees buckled. A woman started crying.

Rowe took aim at one of the cameras and fired two rounds, missing, before he shot out a monitor, scattering glass and shell casings, then leaned over the counter and told the teller: "Git up, ya blood clot, 'fore ah cap you! Don't look at me! Don't touch da fuckin' alahrm, *anybody*, or we fuckin' *kill* you! Gimme da fuckin' money!"

As the man got to his feet and began handing over cash, Lofton went around the back, hauled another teller up, and made her open her drawer. "Everybody back here, get up!" he yelled. "Give us the money, and no fucking dye bombs!

Rowe and Lofton went up and down either side of the counter, stuffing bills into their bag and satchel.

"You blokes want any fuckin' wallets or rings?" O'Hara shouted.

"No," Rowe said.

"Why not?"

"Don't have *time* for dat shit, mon." He grabbed some more money, leaving his gun close by on the counter so he could better see the bills and avoid a grenade. "I *told* you," he said to the teller, squinting through the eye-holes, "just the big ones. And don't *look* at me. Keep your fucking head down!" His patois was inconsistent. "Who got da combination to da safe? Who's da manager?"

"It is time-locked." From his voice, the East Indian teller was a Trinidadian or something, who'd know dialects. "We cannot open it."

O'Hara tried to grab somebody coming in who managed to turn and run, and shot at him twice through the glass of the swinging second door.

In the confusion and screaming, the teller reached over and grabbed the Glock off the counter. Rowe, his peripheral vision impaired, took a wild swing as the teller brought the gun up, then went down for cover and yelled for assistance.

There were four reports from Lofton's Beretta. The man was hit in the chest and throat as he whirled backwards, spraying blood.

"Let's get out of here!" Rowe yelled.

O'Hara was shouting at people who were half-up or trying to crawl, while Lofton ran around the counter to the injured teller and picked up the gun.

Outside, Lofton slipped on the rainy walk as he tried to avoid the wounded man on the pavement, and went down heavily. Money flew from his satchel. Bystanders in the parking lot watched Rowe stop to pick up some bills while Lofton got to his feet and limped to the car. Their heads were still covered when they climbed into the Subaru.

"Get down," Rowe said hoarsely, stepping on the gas.

"They'll be looking for three people." He sideswiped a car pulling in, and barely slowed down as he veered around the corner and ran the red light.

"My ankle's fucked up," Lofton said as he pulled off the mask, his face sweaty. "How the fuck did he get your gun?" Rowe didn't answer. "And why the fuck did *you* start shooting outside?"

"He was getting away," O'Hara said from the back. "Fuck you, man."

Rowe squinted as he gripped the wheel. Ahead, in the distance, he saw flashing lights in the oncoming traffic. Easing off the gas as he moved into the right lane, he said, "Cops. Stay down."

Lofton groaned. "My fucking ankle."

The cruiser hit the siren briefly, then sped by in silence with the panel of lights revolving.

"That was a fucking massacre," Lofton said, fumbling for a cigarette. "I think you killed that guy outside too."

"Stay down," Rowe said. "More cops."

They took the 401 to the Don Valley Parkway, then went south to Bloor. Rowe drove further east and turned up Broadview to an outdoor municipal lot with an automatic ticket dispenser and no camera. There, they split a take of $7,820.

The car was wiped down and the cigarette butts removed. Rowe and Lofton wanted to dump the guns, but Robert said he had to return them to his father's cache. Lofton asked if he could hold onto the Beretta for a couple of weeks, and argued that it was a matter of self-defense until O'Hara finally said all right, what the fuck, maybe just while the heat was on.

They put their hats and gloves into a garbage can and walked separately to the Broadview station, ignoring one another on the platform. O'Hara went south at Yonge, Lofton continued west to Bathurst, and Rowe took the Spadina-University line up to Yorkdale Shopping Centre to retrieve his car.

12

The teller had been found dead at the scene, while the man shot outside the front door died later in hospital. The double homicide drew media coverage for the remainder of the week, so the fact that O'Hara's mother's house hadn't been searched seemed to confirm for Rowe that the guns weren't registered, unless the police had interviewed his father in jail or raided a biker clubhouse somewhere. Despite the discretion imposed on journalists in matters of race, a West Indian accent had been reported in one of the papers. Rowe didn't get much sleep and kept a low profile in the days following the robbery, but was soon drinking his anxiety away publicly.

Lion on the Beach was styled after a pub except for the rock groups, or so he surmised, having associated English-type watering holes with an incongruous mix of red-nosed grand-parents and college-age kids, worn carpeting, tactless lighting, and, if anything, folk music. He preferred darker places.

The band was playing radio standards in a corner of the room that had been cleared of tables, in front of a brass railing that bordered the upper back section. Older singles congregat-ed in the area alongside the bar. There was a dartboard, and a picture of a horse on a post by the partition he was leaning against, his attention divided between the makeshift dance floor and the man with the blonde hair and windbreaker he'd some-how ended up bullshitting with about the perfect robbery.

"You wouldn't want to do a bank," the guy said. "With all the security cameras and everything? What you'd want to do is an art theft."

Rowe turned to him. "You've got to be kidding. You can't move that shit for fifteen years, and only then with contacts."

Beach Boy shrugged as he lifted his draught glass. Wiping his mouth, he leaned in closer. "Just go in through the roof to avoid the sensors—two guys, you'd need two guys to do it. You wouldn't do it for fast cash, you'd think of it as an investment for the future. A retirement fund."

"What roof are we talking about?"

He looked uncertain. "I might know a place."

"Where?"

"I don't want to say right now. But I've checked the angles."

"Well, is it a public gallery or a private collection?"

"Private."

Rowe lit a cigarette. "What kind of artwork?"

"A lot of Group of Sevens, especially A.Y. Jackson."

"If it looks like an inside job, you'd probably be a suspect."

Beach Boy shook his head. "Wouldn't be an inside job. I'd need another guy to help me move the paintings because there are sixteen of them. The sensors cut across the doorway diagonally, right?" He illustrated the plane with his arm. "There are two of them. That's why it'd be best to go in through the roof."

Rowe had seen him as sort of a windsurfer going to seed, but looked at him again. Squaring his shoulders, he took a drag and watched the band. "So how would you get in through the roof? Is there a skylight or some kind of ductwork you could crawl through?"

"No."

"What then? Is it a house or a small building?"

Beach Boy took a sip and said, "Look, you know what the best thing to do would be? Just drive your car up to the place, break in, get in and out. Two guys. Have a few beers first, then bam—set off the alarm and pack the pictures in the trunk fast—no, rent a *van*, then get the hell out before the police show up. That's all you've really got to do. Think about it. It's simple."

"Well, you don't need two people," Rowe said, losing interest. "If you do it yourself you won't have to split it, and there will be one less person to talk about it."

"I guess."

Downstairs, one of the bulbs in the washroom was out. Rowe observed the play of shadows in the mirror as he ran a hand through his bristly hair. Outside the door he paused by the staircase to look at a charcoal collage of rock star faces mounted behind glass on the wall under a light. He didn't know anything about art, but always stopped to study the near-photographic detail.

An older blondish woman half-stumbled out of the ladies' room. Although Rowe stepped aside so she could get by, she stopped to study the picture, and smiled up at him. "Hey, you're cute."

She was squinting as if to steady her wobbly eyes. Her silly expression had a guilelessness he found promising as he took in her wide mouth, and observed that her complexion was fairly unlined in the harsh lighting.

"Thanks. You too." As she was turning to go, he asked, "What's your name?"

"Bella."

"I'm Derek."

"Hi, Derek."

Rowe followed her erratic trip up the staircase. A bit heavy in the trunk, maybe. When they reached the top, he asked, "Do you dance?"

She gave him a coquettish glance. "Sometimes."

"Feel like it now?"

"Sure, why not?"

He took her by the elbow and guided her around the corner of the bar, past the stools, the drinkers in the aisle, the amplifiers and musicians. Bella bumped against a couple of people when they maneuvered onto the dance floor, but moved into the right rhythm as Rowe caught her by the waist to steady her balance. Periodically, he leaned in to talk to her, trying to assess her beyond the giddy drunkenness and pale yellow sweater. He winked over her shoulder as Beach Boy raised a glass to him.

Afterwards, he suggested they go somewhere else, and waited while she went to find her coat and say goodbye to her girlfriend. Leaning against a tabletop near the front, he watched a game of darts until she reappeared wearing a fur jacket. Couldn't locate the friend.

Rowe nodded to the bouncer on their way out the door, and held her arm as they crossed the street to the south side.

He took her to a place called Lido's, but it was too noisy and full of kids to talk properly, so they left and cut back to another one called The Beach Bar. Without a band or dance floor it was comparatively empty.

He bought a vodka and tonic for himself, talked her into a large Coke, and asked for a glass of water on the side. Leaning on her elbow, Bella grinned at him from under her bangs and asked, "So how old are you?"

"Forty-four."

She looked comically agog. "I thought you were younger."

"How about you?"

"Forty-seven."

"I thought *you* were younger."

She shook her head and turned serious. "Hey, d'ya smoke?"

Rowe gave her a cigarette and tapped out another for himself, then looked in his pockets for a light.

"Great. Nobody smokes anymore." Exhaling, she examined the advertisement on the back of his matches. "You don't go to this place, do you? It's disgusting."

"Why?"

"It's a meat market."

"It's just a neighbourhood bar to me."

"You live up there? Me too." Strands of her hair over-lapped, mussed and childlike. "I have a house on Balliol. You live in a house or apartment?"

"Apartment."

"Ever been married?"

"No."

"Why?"

"Guess I never met the right woman."

"You're not bisexual or anything, are you?"

"Not me." Rowe took a drink. "If you're worried about AIDS, I got checked last month and have a clean bill of health at home." While she seemed to be thinking it over, he said, "Here, have some more Coke."

They left the bar fifteen minutes later. As they walked along the sidewalk, she asked, "Do you drive?"

"Not tonight."

"Well, I've got a car up Queen there, but I don't know if I should. I was supposed to stay at my girlfriend's tonight...." Bella buttoned her jacket. Though her articulation had improved, her walk was still unsteady. "You got a license?"

"Yeah, but I've been drinking for a while too, and I've already been charged with Impaired. Let's just catch a streetcar."

"A *streetcar*?" She looked at him as if he was joking. "I haven't been on the TTC in ten years."

"Then it's high time."

The tracks ran by ice cream parlors, confectioneries, bars and restaurants with closed patios. The stores dealing in roller blades and wind surfing were probably dead in the daytime now that it was off-season for the beach and boardwalk. The tourists were gone. The nights continued to get cooler.

There were only a few people on the streetcar. West, past Woodbine, the neighbourhood near the torn-down racetrack was fairly barren until the brief oasis of a mall and neon-lit

kitchenware store renting out of a small building at the junc-
tion of Kingston Road, where the housing and businesses
became increasingly poorer. They passed tattooists, hair stylists,
donut shops, an adult video outlet, the odd used car lot, and
fly-by-night operations with an occasional hand-painted sign.

Sitting to the rear of the side doors, Rowe started kissing
Bella. She still looked alright, but now he wasn't sure why he'd
thought she was younger. "How come I never saw you in that
bar before?" she asked.

"I haven't been going there very long."

"It's not a bad place. Gone to bed with anybody there
yet?"

A trick question, but he was encouraged by her cockeyed
expression. "Yeah, but it was a fluke. I bumped into this hammered woman I'd been talking to earlier, and said, 'Shall we
leave then?' I was kidding, but she went, 'All right,' and we
walked out the door.

"She lived in a building a little ways away, but when we
got there she realized she didn't have her keys. The front
door was unlocked, but we spent about twenty minutes
banging on her apartment for her twelve-year-old daughter
to wake up and let us in. We were sitting on the stairs when
the girl came in behind us. Turned out *she* had the keys, and
was staying at a friend's place where her mother was supposed to pick her up."

"God."

"Later, I was lying in bed when she had to get up to go to
the washroom. After she came back, the daughter—who had-
n't gone to sleep yet—stuck her head around the corner and
saw me there, and started shouting, 'Mother, I want to talk to
you in the hall, right *now*! Mother, come out here *now*.' So she
went out in her nightie, and I could hear the girl yelling,
'Mother, what do you think you're doing? You're drunk, and
you don't even *know* him!'"

"Roles were, like, reversed."

"Yeah. She was still up watching TV at five when I had to sneak out past her."

"Shit. You don't have any kids, do you?"

"'No. What about you?"

"Married twice, no kids." Bella smiled, looking out the window. "Somehow I got away with writing children's books, though. I was considered quite the freaking expert."

He put his arm around her. "How'd you get into that?"

"A long time ago I got up the guts to take some stories I'd written to a publisher, and the vice president said, 'These are the *worst* children's stories I've ever read.'" She laughed. "I guess he figured I had talent but didn't like the material, because he hired me to write this series on manners instead. I also wrote jacket copy and whatever else was required, you know, like this project called *Questions Kids Ask*, and then there was an encyclopedia . . . we had to sit around a board-room and come up with over a thousand questions a five-year-old might ask, and would get pretty punchy late at night, starting out with, 'Why is the grass green? Why is the sky blue?' and end up with 'Do chickens have lips?' It was tough going in with a hangover and having to explain the mating habits of the duckbilled platypus or whatever. I knew I could make up almost anything and have kids believe me if I wrote it with authority."

"You still write?"

"No . . . I went freelance after that for a while since the job had been just for the manners thing. They didn't have any in-house writers."

Rowe hadn't counted on an intellectual. "I guess they could tell you had breeding, to pick you to do manners."

"Yeah. I turned into a fucking manners *expert*," she said. "After that I saw this ad in the paper for someone to teach etiquette classes for children, and phoned to tell them about these books I'd written, and got the job. It was at this institute that'd been started by these women who were already running a modeling agency. They decided to expand the courses to include subjects like, um . . . 'Lifestyle Teaching.'

"One student's mother was a columnist for the *Sun*, and thought my class was interesting enough to write about, and then another reporter followed up with a big story a few weeks later. I said that I'd come by my social graces early; while other parents were reading the usual bedtime stories to their kids, my mother was instructing us from, like, Emily Post. I said the class filled a gap in today's society when you thought about all the families with two jobs, where the parents didn't have time to teach their kids the ins and outs of etiquette, but still wanted them to know how to behave. Oh—and I told how there was this little girl who was always making fun of another kid's hair, I think it was, so I took her aside and explained why it wasn't nice to mock the way anyone looked. So, like, she was gazing into my face so attentively during my spiel, and when I asked her if she had any questions, she wanted to know why I had so many grey things in my teeth."

"Priceless."

"Can you believe it? So then this radio station in L.A. somehow picked up the story. They got my number from the second writer and called for an interview. A news service broadcast it across Canada, the States, Australia and New Zealand, and I started getting calls from radio stations all over North America. I remember this uptight asshole with a British accent from a Victoria station asking me, 'How do the children respond to you as an etiquette expert? Are they intimidated by you at all?'

"'No, not really,' I said. 'Once they realize I'm not some old biddy with a pickle up my posterior, they're okay.' He didn't seem to like that, and broke for a commercial.

"Calgary gave me a hard time. The guy was nice enough to me pre-interview during the sound check, but as soon as he got me on the air live he tried to burn me, saying, 'You certainly don't sound like an etiquette expert.'

"I shot back, 'I guess you could say that Doctor Ruth Westheimer doesn't look like a sex expert.' That shut him up. There was dead air for five or ten seconds, then he sort of warmed up a bit."

Rowe said, "You're famous, then."

"No . . . I didn't have a book or anything to plug to compensate for my time, so the novelty started wearing thin after a while. When I moved I got an unlisted number. A couple of months later, Channel Nine tracked me down through the institute and asked me to be on a show about kids and manners, but I turned it down."

As the streetcar approached the downtown core, Bella looked out the window at the dingy, two-bit businesses and the flotsam and jetsam from a mission who were hanging around the corner of Sherbourne or lying in the park across the street. "I haven't been on the TTC in ten years," she repeated. "Hey, what did you say your name was again?"

They got off at Yonge and went down into the subway, passing a kid panhandling at the bottom of the stairs. Rowe slid their transfers under the glass of the ticket kiosk and followed her through the turnstile. There were other people on the platform. They walked over to a red bench in the Designated Waiting Area and sat in a pool of light beneath an overhead camera. Opposite, on the tiled wall, there was a mural of the Eaton Centre.

By the time the train hit the St. Clair station, it had been about forty-five minutes since they'd left the last bar. Holding her by the arm as they went up the escalator, he said, "It's only about ten minutes from here."

"We've gotta *walk* now?"

"Unless we see a cab. We're almost there."

On the bridge he stopped to draw her attention to the expanse of black valley and the faintly starry sky, then kissed her to try to recover the giddy, over-aged naïf who'd told him how cute he was. They held hands as they continued along the sidewalk into the familiar district of trees and older, well-to-do homes. Some were covered in ivy, faced by stone or cast in lamp light. East of Mount Pleasant where St. Clair narrowed, the neighbourhood would become more affluent in the maze of streets culminating in a dead-end at the Moore Ravine.

"You're not poor, are you?"

"Look around," he said. "Does this look like a poor area to you?"

"Well, you don't live in a rooming house, do you?"

"No, it's a one-bedroom apartment."

At the traffic light, Bella looked at the three-storey building on the southeast corner with the big antenna on its roof. "Wait—you don't live *there*, do you?"

"Yeah, why?"

"My *lawyer* owns it. This is too much."

They crossed the street. Despite its plain architecture he thought the abundance of hedges and bushes around the property helped present an attractive address, overall. Too bad the flowers seemed to have been dug up. "My *lawyer* owns this place," she said again. "Going out with a guy who lives in one of his buildings. Wow."

Rowe wasn't sure what to make of her tone; she sounded as if she felt she was compromising herself. He gave her rump a slap. "So what's your point? Is he supposed to be a slumlord?"

She waited while he fished out his keys. "I just don't know what he'd think."

The ledge and floor beneath the panel of metal boxes in the small foyer were littered with junk mail. When they walked down the hall, he noticed all the fingerprints on the door to the stairwell.

She seemed to survey his apartment as they hung up their jackets, looking around at the grey sofa and overstuffed armchair, the plants, dinette set and shelving unit with his magazines and paperbacks. A framed poster with the familiar image of a sailor kissing a girl on V-Day hung on the wall near another of a painting of two prize fighters by George Bellows.

Rowe came over with a cellophane bag of marijuana and a bong fashioned from a toilet paper roll, and sat down beside her on the couch. He sprinkled some weed into the aluminum foil bowl and held the short cardboard tube to his mouth, his palm covering the other end while he lit it, then lifted his hand while inhaling.

"Your taste is just so ... *different* from mine," she remarked.

After a moment he said, "Yeah?"

Bella brushed her hair back as she waited for him to refill the pinpricked foil, then took a toke. She coughed and said, "Yeah ... I mean *really*."

"What do you mean?"

"Well, everything. Like this cheap little coffee table, for example. It's just so different from anything I'd ever buy."

Rowe understood that he was being insulted. "Do you want a beer or something?"

"A beer. Okay."

He got up and walked into the kitchen. As he took a bottle from the refrigerator, he heard her talking again. "You just rent this place, right?"

"Uh huh."

"And you're forty-five, right?"

"Forty-four." He twisted off the cap and walked into the living room, skirting the TV rabbit ears. "Why?"

"Wow," Bella said softly. She looked around as she took a sip, and seemed perplexed. "Well, look at this place. You've just fucked your life away, haven't you?"

Rowe couldn't quite believe what he'd heard. It was like a clap of thunder. He looked at her as if for the first time, trying to distinguish idle teasing from this sinister revelation which until now he'd only suspected. A total stranger without any agenda had travelled all this way to be with him, and immediately zeroed in on a fact so elementary that it had to have been obvious to anybody who'd ever visited him and secretly scorned, among other things, the coffee table that he'd assembled from IKEA and since burned with cigarettes.

It also seemed to him that this self-involved cunt had morphed into a monster. He drank some beer. "Say what?"

"Well, really. You've pretty much fucked your life away. You're forty-four, you don't own anything. . . ." She waved her hand. "This is it."

"Well, how did you get your house?" he asked. "You probably married into it."

"No, I'm in real estate."

He thought about it as he raised the bottle again. It was both strange and enlightening. Even though he was all over the news, sort of, he didn't have much to show for it.

"Oh, anyway," she said, brightening, "how many cigarettes do you have? If you can rustle up enough, I'll stay overnight."

Rowe smiled unpleasantly as he stood up. "No, you're going home. I'm calling you a fucking cab."

He walked into his bedroom and was flipping through the telephone book when Bella came in and sat down beside him cheerfully. "Hey, you must be really mad at me. I'm sorry about what I said; it's just the way I am—I'm half German and half Russian. I just have to say whatever comes into my head."

"That's fine," Rowe said, "but you still have to go."

"Wow . . . you probably want to hit me."

He glanced at her as he picked up the phone. "No, I don't give that much of a shit. You were probably right."

"I don't know if I have money for a taxi."

"Well, you'd better start looking, because I'm not giving you any."

13

Jack Lofton saw a doctor about his sprained ankle after his fall outside the bank, and was given a cane. He'd been drinking for days and had taken to carrying the Beretta in his leather jacket with a full clip. His memories were sketchy, but he knew that he'd been refused service at the liquor store for being inebriated, had lost his bandanna, been too drunk to fuck, and that an alarmed tenant in his building, perhaps thinking he was dead, had alerted the superintendent after seeing his legs sticking out from under the stairs where he'd crawled and fallen asleep.

In periods of hung-over clarity he understood that his money was still safe and he hadn't been arrested. Also, that O'Hara's guy died too, and that as far as he knew he hadn't confessed to any strangers or shot anybody else.

After one of his sporadic sleeps and some leftover pizza, Lofton felt comparatively revived and went down to Marva's basement apartment with a bottle of rye, intending to do himself proud before he got into the sauce. He had too much on his mind to stay sober. Sitting on her sofa in a sleeveless black T-shirt, he smoked a cigarette while she talked on the phone from the adjacent chair. He found her barely recognizable when she dressed sloppily and went around without make-up, especially when her hair was knotted up in those rows.

A door down the hall opened, and a white guy came out. Lofton had almost forgotten about the roommate. What a fucked-up arrangement. A greasy-looking character in his late twenties walked past the sheet cordoning off her pretend bedroom, and said hey. He nodded to Marva, who gave him a wave on his way out the door. She kept talking. Lofton got to his feet and took his bottle of Canadian Club into the kitchenette. Aside from a few unwashed dishes, she seemed to keep the place fairly clean and probably wasn't a bad cook if the books and recipes he came across while hunting for a glass were any indication. He flicked his ash into the sink and poured himself a drink with ice and a splash of water. After a long swallow, he freshened it.

When he returned to the living room, Marva said to whoever she was talking to, "Look, I've gotta go now, okay? Right. Okay, see you . . . yeah. Bye." She hung up, and tugged her sweat pants as she crossed her legs. "That was Jacqueline. It doesn't look good about her getting her kids back."

Lofton butted his cigarette. "That's too bad. Listen, this roommate of yours . . . did you say you two ever got together?"

She looked at him in surprise, and laughed. "Tony? *No.* He's not my type at all."

"Why not?"

"Well, I've got higher standards."

Lofton reflected on the implicit compliment. "Well, he must have thought something like that'd probably happen when he moved in. He's at least come on to you, hasn't he?"

"No," she said, looking at him oddly. "Why are you asking? Are you drunk again?"

"No, I'm not *drunk* again."

He hesitated before lifting his glass.

"When Tony moved in, I told him how it had to be. I hardly ever see him."

"It's just a strange set-up, that's all."

"He pays his rent on time. That's all I care about."

After a pause, Lofton nodded to the coffee table and said, "There're some nice pictures there. I like that one of you in the tank top that looks like it was shot in a studio."

Marva glanced over. "Oh, yeah. I had this pile of pictures when I took modelling."

"You were a model?"

"Well, I took a course and got some catalogue work and stuff, but I didn't make enough money to keep doing it."

Lofton had another drink before he got up from the couch and walked over. He didn't feel entirely sure of himself when he sat on her armrest and leaned down to kiss her. She tilted her head without expression but seemed responsive, so he put his hand on the side of her face and Frenched her.

She drew back and touched his chin. "Your beard scratches."

They were going to make it this time. He kissed her more gently as he caressed her through the sweatshirt, expecting a bra, and got a lift from the immediacy of her breasts. Firm showbiz tits on the other side of the NIKE logo. She put her hand over his, cautioning or helping him, it wasn't clear, while he massaged her and tweaked the definition of a large nipple.

Marva turned her head away. "So, are you just playing, or is this serious? It doesn't matter; I just want to know, that's all."

He'd been roller coasting from omnipotence to depression and missed having a real confidant, a woman with whom he could share the same kind of rapport he'd had with his ex. At least before things went bad and she told him she was afraid of him.

"I'm serious," Lofton said, getting off the chair and going onto his knees in front of her. He pulled off her slippers. "I like you a lot."

"What are you—hey!" She laughed and yanked her foot from his hands.

"Relax," he said, and gripped her by the ankle, bringing her leg up. He tried to work as many brown toes as he could into his mouth, and sucked them.

"You're crazy."

The Grim Reaper looked at her over the barbed wire circling Lofton's biceps. Lightning bolted up the insides of his arms as he held her calf, licking her sole and instep. "You need

this," he said with a quaver in his voice, maddeningly susceptible these days to every flitting emotion.

"That tickles," she giggled huskily, wiggling her foot.

"Hold still." He grasped her other ankle and licked
between her toes. Then nibbled the baby for good luck.

"This is the first time for *this*," Marva said.

Lofton got to his feet and took her by the hand.

"Where are we going?"

"You'll see."

He led her down the hall and pushed the sheet aside.
Marva crawled onto the bed beside him and lay down. "You're
not the kind of guy who always wants to have sex, are you?"
Her hand was against his chest as he leaned over her. "Like,
you don't get mad if a girl doesn't want to sometimes, are
you?"

"I don't know." He had to stop her from talking, and
blocked her next query with his mouth. Her arm slowly went
around him. Even though his hands were on her breasts, she
rolled over when the telephone rang. Lofton lowered his zip-
per and adjusted his prick, and watched her face go from half-
dazed and sexy to blank again as she talked in that annoying,
zombie way.

"I got a friend here," she said into the phone. "Remember,
from before?"

He leaned on his elbow and waited.

"Here," she said, holding out the receiver. "It's Tyrone. He
wants to talk to you. When he phoned here yesterday I told
him he shouldn't be calling anymore."

Lofton tensed, and formed a scowl as he moved up against
her and took it. "What the fuck do you want?"

"You better get the fuck outta there, *bitch*, 'fore I be
blowin' you away."

The line wasn't very clear. He hoped Marva couldn't feel
his heartbeat as he saw everything ensnaring him in a vast con-
spiracy of shit. As steady and threatening as possible, he said,

"You're the faggot with the one-inch dick, right? I'm about to fuck somebody the way she *likes* to be fucked, then I'm going to get my Beretta and fucking shoot you a new asshole if you ever fucking call here again. I'm going to ask her right now where you live."

"*Fool*! My posse's gonna waste your white . . ."

Lofton handed the phone back. Marva laughed incredulously as she hung up. "With the one-inch *dick*? I could not *believe* what you were saying!" Then, remembering to take it off the hook, she turned over and said, "And you're going to shoot him a new *what*?"

He got up to take a leak, then find his drink and cigarettes. Maybe that would be the end of Tyrone, but he doubted it. Having finished most of his rye and water, Lofton walked slowly into the kitchen to refill his glass, and then crossed the hall to find that she'd gone to the washroom herself. He eased onto her bed without spilling anything, and looked at her rack of dresses and the hats on the overhead hooks. He could be shot to death as easily in a cramped basement in Parkdale as anywhere else. Could be, motherfucker Ty-*rone* had hisself a key made, or just had to knock and he'd be inside.

When Marva came in, he leaned on his elbow and asked, "So, where's your ex-boyfriend living now?"

"You mean Tyrone? I don't think he's got a regular address. If he's not at my friend's place, he's still somewhere around Jane and Finch most likely. I don't think he's up there right now, though," she added, stretching out beside him.

"How do you know?"

"He was on his cell. They're probably out cruising or buying crack, or something stupid like that."

Lofton tried to put it out of his mind and get back to business. Taking another drink, he put his glass on her chest of drawers and turned over to kiss her. She was responding less passionately as he put his hand on her side and went under the top, sliding over an outline of ribs to the warmth and curve of her breasts. He was pulling her sweatshirt up over her nipples when Marva stopped him. "Look, I'm sorry, I'm fucked up," she said, adjusting herself. "I . . . I don't know if you want to forget me and go home or what, but I find sex disgusting."

Lofton sat up and reached for his glass. "Jesus fucking *Christ.*"

She looked at him defiantly.

"What *is* this shit? The first time, you told me you wished we weren't doing it."

"That's because nothing works out if it happens right away. I explained why."

"You seemed all right the other times," he said, "when I wasn't drunk, I mean. Were you just faking it, or what?"

"No. Never. How can you ask that?"

He was at a loss. She was too much. He lit a smoke and decided to start drinking seriously.

"I think I'm going to be a prostitute," Marva said. "That's all guys seem to want anyway. . . ."

"You're saying you did come with me, though. At least once you had an orgasm."

"Yes!"

"So then what do you mean, you find it 'disgusting'?"

She sat up and folded her arms. "I might as well start making money since my relationships are always fucked up. I didn't want to go out with black guys anymore because they're so unreliable, but with everyone there's the same shit. And look how you were talking about me to Tyrone."

The rye was sluggishly alleviating his hangover. After another couple to stabilize him for the road, he'd be gone. "I was insulting him—obviously. He was threatening to fucking kill me."

There was a short silence. "So, how were you going to shoot him?" she asked. "You were just kidding, right?"

He took a weary drag from his cigarette. "Baby, I never kid."

"So, have you got a gun or what? Because he does."

"Maybe."

She was skeptical. Lofton took in her dark eyes and wide nose, her broad cheekbones and the thick lips. She certainly seemed different with her hair in those funky ghetto twists. There was something definitely not right about a stripper wearing sweats and playing virgin. "Do you want to see?" he asked patiently. "First pour me another drink with ice, a third water. And bring the bottle. *Please.*"

When she padded off to the kitchenette, Lofton got up and walked to the closet. He liked the leather fragrance of the coats. As he reached into the pocket of his spiked jacket he considered a shoulder holster, or one that strapped around his ankle in case he was frisked. But then he'd need baggy pants, and it'd still be too hard to draw if some faux Ice T tried to take him out.

He wasn't going to hang around much longer, no matter what she was angling for. His nerves were too uneven with all the bullshit going on. There was a feeling that gangstas were going to be at the door any minute.

Twenty minutes later, with his rye in a bag beneath one arm, Lofton went down her dark driveway between the houses with his cane. He wasn't drunk, but he wasn't feeling as much pain in his leg either.

As he neared the sidewalk he noticed some black males in a vehicle by the curb farther down the block. He couldn't make out the details without looking directly at them, and felt for the Beretta while he headed north towards King, glancing over his shoulder as he crossed the street for the cover of parked cars. He made it to the other side before they pulled out into the road behind him. Lofton recognized what appeared to be a type of assault weapon poking out the window as they accelerated. He dropped awkwardly to the sidewalk behind a minivan, breaking his bottle as the air was cracked by a succession of bullets raking the cars and shattering glass above him.

He lay there, soaked but uninjured. Shards fell from his jacket as he got up and limped to the middle of the road, firing off three rounds at the speeding car.

He caught his breath. His heart was hammering. The noise was still ringing in his head as he put the gun in his pocket and went back for his cane. People were at their windows. He tried to calm himself as he continued in the same direction along Spencer at a stilted clip, wondering if he should ditch the Beretta before he got searched. Neighbours would probably see him if he went back into Marva's, and he was sober enough to know that he'd get fucked up going the opposite way. As far as he could remember, the small streets inevitably ended up at the Gardiner Expressway and Lake Shore Boulevard. Somewhere there was a bridge over to Sunnyside Beach, but he couldn't remember where. The area was heavily policed and would be swarming with cops any minute now.

Nobody up at King seemed to have been downed by a stray bullet, but he could hear shouting and see people running around, maybe because the car had barely made the corner. What he had to do, and fast, was grab a cab up to the Bloor subway line or catch a streetcar east, then get shit-faced in a bar closer to home.

14

A couple of hours later, Rowe was sitting in his chair watching TV when his telephone rang. From the faint connection and street noise, he gathered without having understood what was said that Lofton was outside his building, and buzzed him in.

It took Lofton almost fifteen minutes to get up the stairs and down the hall. Then he was at the door, swaying on his cane with eyes that seemed to be having difficulty focusing.

"You're hammered," Rowe said.

"Fuck. You got a beer?" He lurched and then caught his balance, wobbling.

"How about a Coke?"

"*Fuck.*" Lofton's scorn was dramatic. "Beer . . . *please.* You don't have *any* fuckin' idea. . . ." He made it around the coffee table to the sofa, and sat down heavily as his cane hit the carpet.

Rowe, sizing up the situation, went into the kitchen and took a couple of beers from the refrigerator. Perhaps he'd get Lofton to a bar instead of having an unmanageable drunk on his hands all night. Make use of his impromptu sociability.

"I can't figure this show out," he said, nodding to the television as he handed him the bottle. "It's shot like a documentary and looks real enough, but nobody being videotaped ever asks, 'Hey—what's with the fucking lights and camera?' And they never try to cover their faces, they just keep crying and screaming and pleading with the police."

He sat in the armchair and aimed the remote to lower the volume. "I mean, everybody in North America's got to know the show by now, but nobody ever looks at the camera and says, 'Wait a minute—I'm not on *Cops*, am I?' I'd think it'd be something to find yourself on national TV during one of your darker moments. Even if they paid you a bundle later to use the embarrassing footage, you'd think your initial reaction to the lights and camera in your face would be surprise."

"Editing," Lofton mumbled.

"If it's been cut out where it's explained to them why they're being videotaped, they should still be sneaking glances or trying to improve their behaviour, but they seem completely oblivious. And it's definitely not a hidden camera."

"Almost got fucking . . . *killed* tonight," Lofton said.

"What?"

"Fucking . . ." Lofton struggled for the appropriate words. "Fucking drive-by. Niggers tried to shoot me outside Marva's—*fuck*. I shot too, but missed, I think."

Rowe turned down the TV volume. "Are you telling me you were in a gun fight?"

Lofton stared without appearing to see him. "Fucking . . . yeah, homeboy. Broke my fucking bottle."

"What have you been drinking, anyway?"

"Rye, *Mother*. Tequila."

"This the ex-boyfriend?"

"Marva's old boyfriend. I was gone . . . fucking *gone*, man."

Rowe took a swig of beer and turned back to the television while Lofton fumbled to light a cigarette. It was impossible to know what to believe. "I'm just on my way up to Originals. You should come with me."

"Fucking leg hurts." Lofton slowly got to his feet and unbuckled his belt. Squinting with a smoke in his mouth, he started to pull his Levis down.

"What are you doing?"

His jeans were around his knees when he said, "Look."

"Pull your fucking pants up."

Lofton stood there swaying. "I'm just *telling* you . . . fuck."

Rowe stood up and tried to guide him back to the sofa. "You're going to fall into the TV."

"Man . . ." Lofton looked in his direction with a hurt expression. "I wouldn't do anything . . . you don't have to worry, I wouldn't—" He bumped into the coffee table and almost lost his balance, then went down hard on the couch. His cigarette bounced, sending sparks into the carpet. "*Fuck.*"

Rowe bent down and handed him the smoke. "All right, look, we're both going out now to have some fun. The fresh air will wake you up. Just fix your pants." He put his arm around Lofton's shoulder to try to ease him off the sofa enough to pull up his jeans by a belt loop, but he was uncooperative and reached past him for the bottle. He was very heavy.

Rowe sighed and walked back around the coffee table. He turned off the television. As he watched him slowly struggling with his pants, he realized he was in the presence of a blackout. Even if Lofton had had the faculties to find his way there and was more or less keeping up his side of the conversation, he was going to be missing hours from his life as if they'd never happened. Unless they went out and did something, Rowe himself was going to be sucked into that black hole. There was also a concern that Lofton might piss himself. He could put the man's head into the toilet bowl, and he wouldn't even remember being there.

"Fucker had some fuckin' . . . *uzi* or something," Lofton said, pulling things out of his pockets. He stood there with his pants open around his hips, looking at a wad of crinkled twenties and fifties.

"What are carrying all that money for? You're going to lose it."

Lofton looked up at him, then down again.

"Do you want me to hold onto it?" Rowe asked. "You're just going to lose it all." He stood up and took the bundle. Rifling through the bills, he counted four hundred and sixty, and took out three twenties. "Hold onto this. I'll give you back the rest tomorrow." He watched Lofton pocket the money with difficulty. "All right—zip up, drink your beer, and we're out of here."

After Lofton finished off the bottle and they managed to get his loose-fitting jeans into place, he was slowly ushered out the door. When they got into the stairwell, however, he refused to move. It wasn't clear why. He stood leaning on his cane with his back to the wall. Rowe looked up from the landing and said, "Come on, man—let's *go*."

Lofton shook his head.

"What are you waiting for? You're on the stairs. We have to leave the building. Then we're going to catch a cab to a bar."

Lofton didn't answer. He pulled open the door to the hall-way and turned right, apparently trying to get back into the apartment. The door closed again. Rowe waited. When he saw Lofton's image pass the glass in the other direction, he went down the rest of the steps to the first floor and walked along the corridor to meet him at the bottom of the north staircase.

Lofton seemed surprised to see him when he got to the landing, and turned around gripping the railing as he climbed back to the second floor. Rowe walked down the hall and waited outside the first stairwell. Nothing happened, so he went up to find him leaning against the wall again. "What the fuck are you doing? Let's go. Come *on*."

There was no answer. Lofton looked angry and confused.

Rowe beckoned with his finger. "Come on. Let's go get some more beer."

It was another fifteen minutes before he managed to coax Lofton down the stairs. Outside, on the northeast corner, Rowe tried to sober him up while looking for a taxi. He did-n't want to drive for fear of Lofton throwing up. It was stupid taking him to a bar, but at least he'd be able to keep an eye out for a woman at the same time. It wouldn't be the first time he'd had to keep him propped up.

Lofton was getting increasingly difficult to deal with. From his drunken muttering it seemed he was starting to see Rowe as his antagonist. Screwing his face into his most disgusted scowl, Lofton gave him a half-hearted push.

"Relax." Rowe saw a southbound cab and hailed it. The driver flicked on his indicator and slowed down to make a U-turn, but as he pulled around to the curb he suddenly hit the gas when Lofton began swinging his cane.

"You scared him off. Fucking *behave* yourself," Rowe said, staying out of range. He moved forward and grabbed the cane, twisting it downwards to subdue him. "Now just stand here and don't do anything."

"*Ffffuck!*" Lofton pulled away, and with both hands on the handle, began jabbing him.

Rowe knocked it aside and pushed him hard, then turned and walked back towards his building. He looked over his shoulder expecting to see Lofton coming after him, but he was sprawled on the sidewalk. Trying to prop himself up, he pulled a gun from his jacket and aimed it in Rowe's direction, but fell back again.

There was a car waiting at the lights across the intersection, but the driver and passenger were talking and didn't seem to be paying attention. Traffic was going by steadily. Rowe ran back, giving Lofton a wide berth, and picked up the Beretta. He looked at his partner on the sidewalk by the park, soaked in urine, bringing down real estate values. He was either going to kill someone or get them all arrested.

Rowe glanced around before putting a steel toe into Lofton's gut. As he walked east under the trees, he decided that he wasn't going to give him his money back. And now he was going to have to go and ditch the gun in the Moore Park ravine in the fucking dark.

15

After passing over replies to her personal ad from a convict in Kingston Penitentiary, an elderly man in a trailer camp, and a two hundred pound individual named Emillio who said he loved to 69 and *make many wimmen bery, bery hot*, Patricia Meredith contacted someone who worked in the book trade and said that he shared her appreciation for candlelit dinners, children and long walks. Judging from his photograph, he looked presentable.

Her ad had described her as an attr 32-yr-old artisan & mother. During their phone conversation she'd elaborated on the subject of her daughter, Kelly, and the craft business she operated out of her house making ashtrays, candy dishes and small bowls, which she fashioned from aluminum and sold on consignment to small stores. This line of work had begun sometime after she'd earned an M.A. in Geography and had accumulated thousands in loans from the government, on the advice of a friend who sold pottery and rented a stand at an annual crafts fair.

The balance between his sort of rugged looks and involvement with books intrigued her, as her submissive role in S&M circles revolved to some extent around the same dichotomy: men who could mete out punishment with a sensibility that could appreciate the subtleties of restraint when required.

They'd had a promising talk. Derek Rowe seemed reasonably intelligent as he discussed career objectives in the area of management, and he enjoyed reading—well, crime, westerns and political thrillers, but at least he read. As for movies, he liked Tarantino but professed to share an interest in foreign films such as *La Femme Nikita*.

Cigarettes were a vice, unfortunately, but there didn't seem to be a problem with drugs or alcohol, so she could worry about breathing the secondhand smoke later. He sounded fit enough with the horseback riding and white water rafting and whatever else he'd said he did. She was too lazy for all that outdoor activity herself, but he'd probably be all right joining Kelly and herself at the community pool, or ordering Chinese and settling in with a video when babysitters were a problem. Thankfully, there was no baggage like a separation or children.

She didn't want to give out her address just yet, so it was agreed that they'd meet in the Lava on College not far from her home. Patricia put on lipstick and a touch of mascara, clipped her auburn hair, and picked out a purple wide-brimmed hat to go with her long dress, scarf, and the funky coat she'd bought secondhand. Her eyes were as blue as cornflowers as she checked herself in the hall mirror and brushed off some lint.

She called Kelly, and had to repeat herself twice before the girl got off her bed and sighed her way up the basement stairs, always resentful when she had to spend the night at Arlene's and Mario's. They left by the rear door and walked past the backyard tool shed that she'd remodeled into a work studio, and opened the gate.

A man she presumed to be Derek motioned her over to a table on the upper level to the right of the bar. In the orange-reddish lighting he looked older and rougher around the edges. The hair was now quasi-military, and greyer. The tight Levi's also dated him, as did the *Miami Vice* T-shirt-and-jacket ensemble.

"Hello," he said, pulling out a chair.

"Hi." She took off her coat and hat.

After she was seated, he sat down opposite her. "Nice place. Is this your local hang-out?"

"I don't go to bars very much anymore," Patricia said mildly. "I don't like it when men come up and bother you to dance, or try to talk. I just want to tell them to . . ." she shrugged with a small laugh, "fuck off."

His smile was ambiguous. "I thought that was why they put dance floors in these places. Where do you prefer to meet people, besides ads?"

"I've always thought the best way was through friends, or at a party."

"A party—well, sure." He looked around. "It's probably faster to get a drink at the bar. What would you like?"

"Maybe a Carlsberg if they have it."

Patricia watched him walk through the narrow main section alongside some couches and an exposed brick wall with mounted speakers. Doors to a closed patio were set within yellow enclaves, rimmed with white bulbs and decorated above by stained glass. Fans revolved on the red ceiling. The crowd looked younger than last time, maybe in their early twenties, but the ambiance with the angular counters, light shades and fixtures remained neo-Art Deco. Behind her, along the wall, there was an array of geometric mirrors.

When Derek came back he placed a glass and bottle on the table in front of her. "I guess you don't come here that often then."

"I've been here with my friend a few times, once when she was here to read her poetry." Pouring some beer, she added, "I don't think you're allowed to smoke in this area." Derek glanced around and put the pack back in his jacket. "Margaret's a good poet. She's a radical feminist, so most of her poetry is heavily political."

"She a lesbian?"

Patricia laughed lightly. "Well . . . yes, as a matter of fact."

"Right." He reached for his glass. "From what I can see, if a woman fifteen years ago said she wasn't a feminist it was like admitting she was a moron. Now, with a lot of things like equal pay out of the way, the hardcore types seem to have hijacked the whole thing."

"I consider myself a feminist," she said.

"Well, all right. But you're not a 'radical' feminist. If you were, you probably wouldn't be sitting here with me."

She let it go, and felt him watching her as she sipped her beer, looking out the window. Perhaps to get back on track he said it was nice she was able to work on her art while raising a daughter, and asked how she got into it with a degree in Geography. She told him she couldn't get a job teaching without a Ph.D. and had to repay thirty thousand dollars in student loans. It was too much debt to stay in university, especially after she and her husband split up and she left Windsor. They'd used a lot of the money to live on. When asked what he did, she said that her ex used to sing with a punk band but gave it up after receiving an inheritance from his grandmother. He was living in her old house.

After a brief silence, Derek inquired about her interest in working with metal. Patricia told him about her friend who was into pottery and always had a booth at the One-Of-A-Kind show at Exhibition Place, and said she was planning to rent space next year as well.

When she finished her beer, he ordered another round. She excused herself to go to the washroom. Walking through the throng of strangers milling about the bar, she admired the two kitschy lava lamps standing among the martini glasses on a shelf behind the bottles: globular and psychedelic. There was red lighting over the far hallway by another wall of mirrors.

Even if he wasn't intellectual or artistic, he seemed normal enough, except perhaps for the reactionary attitude. She wondered what Margaret or Arlene would think. Trouble was, you couldn't always go by a lesbian's opinion in these matters, and Arlene generally had something nasty to say about everyone, including own her husband, whose hygiene was a handicap in bed. They'd still have to admit that she could do a lot worse, if they had any real idea what the personals could dredge up.

When she got back, Derek asked her to dance to a Cranberries song. She wasn't always comfortable on the floor, but he seemed to know what he was doing, even if he'd learned some of his moves in the disco era. She found she was enjoying herself enough that she could overlook the aftershave.

Back at the table he held out her chair. "So, have you met a lot of men through your ad?"

"Not really. I was seeing somebody else for a little while. He had a mean streak, and my daughter didn't like him. Unfortunately, I have to see him again because I owe him some money."

"For what?"

"He lent me two hundred dollars."

"Maybe he wasn't all bad."

"He was," she said with quiet resolve. "He told Kelly that he thought my—my *ass* was getting too fat. He didn't like fat asses."

"Oh. Well, we know he was blind anyway."

"Maybe he had a point, but I don't think you say that to somebody's child. She's very unforgiving; she'll just cut you off. It'd be tough to be her friend."

"She's eleven, right?"

As they were talking, she concluded that Derek was promising, even if he didn't quite match his photo and was less than enlightened. Perhaps with his background in the book trade he had a working knowledge of the Marquis de Sade. It was probably a good idea to have sent Kelly away for the night.

16

The telephone brought Jack Lofton out of a fitful sleep that had been broken earlier by a hangover that he'd subdued with two shots of tequila and an aspirin. The digital radio clock said 9:47. He made it to the bottom of the sofa-bed and picked up the receiver. "Yeah?"

"So, you're *there*."

He lay on his back and opened one eye again. Near the top of the wall behind him, light was coming through the curtains inside the window ledge. "Hi."

"I've been calling," Marva said, "but apparently you're never home."

"I've been kind of busy."

There was a half-hearted laugh. "I thought you were dead or something. I heard the gunshots the other night, and got a call from Tyrone who said that he and his friends were blasting you. And you were shooting too? I could not *believe* it. The police were around, knocking on doors, but I said I didn't know anything."

The off-white walls around him had a bluish tint that reminded him of a gas station washroom, though the cupboards over the sink in the kitchenette were a modern design of fake wood, and the counter and stainless steel sink looked new. But now, lying naked and a little sick, he saw his bachelor apartment as a cell with a puke green carpet.

"So, what's going on?" she asked. "You didn't get shot or go to the hospital or anything?"

"No, your friends can't aim."

"I think you hit their mirror."

He reached up to the small table behind the TV for a can of stale beer, but it was empty. "One of the side mirrors?"

"I don't know, but I think they're still gunning for you."

Checking another can, he tasted ash as a butt floated against his lips.

"So, why haven't you phoned?"

He wiped his mouth as he went back on one elbow. "I don't know. . . . Maybe we shouldn't see each other for a while."

"What? Why—because of Tyrone?"

"No, it's just not working out. The hassles you give me about sex—"

"Because of *sex*? You would break up with me because of that? I never would have believed you were like that." Whether there was some kind of stupid religious conflict at work or she'd been telling the truth about being fucked up, he didn't care. Not with a posse trying to put a bullet in him when he didn't even know where his own gun was. "I used to get into trouble for wanting sex *too* much," she said.

As long as she didn't think he was afraid to see her. After he hung up, Lofton crossed the few feet of carpet to the tile that marked the boundary of the kitchen, and went into the tiny bathroom to the left of the refrigerator.

He was flushing the toilet when the telephone rang. He knew it was Marva again. When he picked it up she asked if he was really serious about not seeing her anymore. Lofton sat on the edge of his bed and tiredly advised her not to play head games with men if she wanted to stay with them.

"You know, I can get even with you—just ask anyone," she said. "I called a guy's wife one time and told her all about him and me. And I once called the po*lice* on a boyfriend and told them he stole my jewellery. They took him to the police station and kept him there for, like, five hours. I could tell them that it was you shooting on the street, and that I saw your gun too."

"If you did that, then they'd have to know about Tyrone, and I don't think he'd be too happy about that."

"I don't care about Tyrone! *Or*," she said, "I could tell Tyrone where you live, if he still wants to find you. If I wanted to."

Her threats were triggering an unexpected response. She was, in effect, showing him that she cared for him. Maybe staying with her would be a notch above getting shot when he walked out his door. Lying back, he closed his eyes and asked, "Why are you even bothering? Obviously it wasn't really working."

"It was okay. I was wondering what you were all about. If you were real or not."

"So you're saying you still want to go out."

There was a pause. "I thought you're saying you don't want to."

"I'm just trying to weigh my options."

"So . . . *you* want to still?"

"Well, maybe, if you still do. But listen, and this is important: I don't give a shit about your ex-boyfriend or his friends, but between the two of us, I had to get rid of my gun, so don't be telling him about me—when I'm over there, or anything like that. I could kick his head off if I had to, but I don't want to be shot at. That would just be fucking stupid, wouldn't it?"

"Yeah, I don't want to have anything to do with him. They're crazy, all of them."

"All right. And maybe it's better if you come over here more, instead of me going there."

"Yeah. So, do you want to come over now, or me go there, or what?"

"Later. I have some appointments first."

After he hung up, Lofton lumbered over to the kitchenette for a beer. There was a *Playboy* calendar and a faded *Clockwork Orange* poster on the wall. Taped to the back of his door was a picture of his favourite superhero, Batman, which he'd carefully cut from a large graphic book with a razor. He regretted having been wasted when he got the Reaper tattoo. It had no doubt seemed appropriate at the time, tongue-in-cheek or otherwise, but it didn't have the philosophical depth of the Dark Knight, whose story, in its purest form, had all the elements of a Greek tragedy. It should have been emblazoned on his shoulder instead. At the end of the day, Bruce Wayne was just a man trying to do the right fucking thing.

As he sat on the edge of the fold-out couch, Lofton looked down at his barbed wire and the lightning zapping up his arms, then at his beer belly and partially swollen penis. He held it at the base and gave it a slow shake, then took a drink. A half-boner for a girl threatening to have him killed because she wanted him. Now that was something special.

17

Rowe was pleased when Patricia called him the next day to let him know that she'd enjoyed their night together. He wasn't quite sure what to make of her soft-spoken intensity and those remote, slightly crossed blue eyes. Her hat conjured the image of a tall, depression-era lady outside a country church. She was a mother from southwestern Ontario after all, but she'd married a punk, and there was that unexpected passive-aggression thing in bed.

She was renting the main floor and basement of a house. There had been dirty dishes, papers and art magazines, dolls, aluminum and various other materials lying around. From a photo on the refrigerator he could see she also wore librarian-type glasses. Most of the furniture was secondhand or even antique, some of it bare wood, some of it with flaking paint. Downstairs in the basement, between the washroom and girl's bedroom, there had been a bookcase with university texts, poetry, feminist journals and medical books like *Our Bodies, Ourselves*, organic healing, something to do with witchcraft, novels about vampires, and nonfiction dealing with sado-masochism and fetishist fashion.

A week later, as he was going through invoices, Rowe thought about Jack Lofton. After letting him sweat for a couple of days he'd let him know that he'd confiscated the gun for having almost been shot, and got rid of it.

Lofton said he'd woken up on a pile of garbage in Chinatown at six in the morning with no recollection whatsoever of having seen Rowe that night. His knuckles were scraped, he was missing his cane, a shoe, his belt, and a few hundred dollars. Although he didn't know how he arrived there, he had a vague sense of being mugged by three Asians, and still claimed that he'd been in a shoot-out in Parkdale.

Rowe was printing up a purchase order when Robert O'Hara walked into the store. For the most part his face had healed. When Rowe told him that he had some returns to ship back to Prentice Hall and Wiley, O'Hara checked his tray in the back room and put his attaché case down. He'd apparently replaced the textbooks he used to carry with issues of *The Financial Post* and stock reports, but Rowe assumed he was packing coke and a gun.

He tore a sheet from the old dot matrix printer and put it aside, then took the purchase binder from the shelf behind him and phoned McGraw-Hill Ryerson. As he was negotiating the steps in the voice mail to reach the trade desk, the second line began ringing. O'Hara picked it up in the other room. Rowe gave the order taker the account number, and looked out the window while she keyed it in. Across the street, sunlight on a house faded as a cloud passed the sun. A thin tree, roped to a metal pole, blew in the wind.

O'Hara came into the room wearing a slick pink and turquoise dress shirt, his hair in a ponytail, and went into the main computer to check the price and availability of *Introduction To The Mathematics Of Demography*.

A little later, Rowe went into the back where O'Hara was cutting down a box, and asked if he'd returned to his apartment yet. O'Hara said he had, but his girlfriend was trying to get him to move for real in case those assholes came back. He'd shown her the Glock and Ruger so she'd stop ragging on him, but swore that he hadn't told her anything about the holdup.

Again, Rowe told him that he should either get rid of the guns they'd used, or keep them stashed off his property. Only after things died down would he bother taking a look for the

Beretta. O'Hara didn't seem overly concerned, and just wanted to know when they were going to do their next bank.

Patricia Meredith made a bookmark for Rowe using a photocopy of an original illustration of Winnie the Pooh with his head in a jar of honey. Underneath was a verse about not knowing which was better: the eating or the anticipation, and on the back she'd written, "To Derek: The Best Honey Eater, Ever."

Despite the gesture she still seemed intellectual to him in a way that wasn't susceptible to his line of talk. For a woman who'd placed a lonely hearts ad and accepted him in her bed that first night, he sensed a resistant undertow that gave him the feeling that he was in uncharted waters. She had university degrees and friends who were dykes and poets, plus she was sort of an artist herself with a vaguely prickly personality.

He was to meet her with a few of her friends at the Black Bull on Queen Street West, where someone's band was playing. Lofton, who'd grudgingly agreed to join him, walked with a slight limp as they approached an older brick building. Period lamps on the patio glowed over nearby motorcycles.

Lofton hung back looking surly when they found the booth where she and her friends were sitting. There were three other women, two of them around forty, and a younger one whose boyfriend was one of the musicians. There wasn't enough room for both of them, so Lofton said he'd go stand at the bar. Rowe, knowing he'd leave, went with him to find another booth.

Patricia looked unusually elegant in a black dress among the bikers, bums, students, arty types and old speed freaks. Rowe saw from the instruments set up by the window that the makeshift stage had been moved since the last time he'd been there, though paintings by local artists still hung on the walls.

"She's good looking," Lofton remarked as he tapped out a cigarette. "She's probably got very lickable feet."

"I haven't gotten around to that."

"You're not into it?"

"I'm into anything if a girl's been in the shower."

Lofton looked around as he exhaled. "I want a woman's feet to smell like feet. Natural. I don't want them smelling like fucking soap."

"I'm into them not smelling like anything." Rowe glanced over his left shoulder at the players at the pool table. The one with the blue hair and red beard had a cobra on his neck. "Want to play a game later?"

"Maybe. Where's the waitress?"

"She'll be around."

"I've gotta get some chips or something."

"Get me a Blue while you're up. I'll get the next round."

Lofton stayed where he was.

"Don't bother. Here she comes."

Ten minutes later, Patricia walked over and sat down beside him. Her breeziness was belied by a curious squint and a note of reproach as she tilted her head and said, "My friends don't think you're being very nice to me."

"There wasn't any room. I couldn't leave Jack with nobody to talk to."

"Don't worry about me," Lofton said.

"Which one of your friends said that?" Rowe asked, looking over at her table.

"Maggie, mostly. She looks out for me."

"Who's Maggie?"

"In the green sweater."

"She looks like butter wouldn't melt in her mouth," Lofton said, in what might have been a put-down or a compliment.

Patricia folded her arms. "I like your tattoos. I almost got one once but I chickened out. I was going to get a butterfly or maybe a bird."

"You want to go to Way Cool Tattoos near Yonge and Wellesley. Ask for Rex, and say Jack sent you." He took a drag, and flicked his cigarette over the ashtray. "He's a fucking artist."

"I don't think I'll do it now. This was back when my husband and the people we hung around with were into that kind of thing."

Rowe was wondering if she was being a bit too friendly with Lofton.

"Hey freaks, what's happening?"

Robert O'Hara was standing behind them with Betty, who looked like a goth Natasha in torn fishnets, and some pencil-necked, leather-clad asexual with short green hair. O'Hara looked wired as he glanced around, snapping his gum. "Hey, there's Rusty." He tossed his hair back and leaned down to Rowe. "I saw those guys on the street tonight. You know, who I had that trouble with."

"Oh? Anything happen?"

"No, I don't think they saw me. It'd be nice if I had a couple of friends with me next time I run into them, or the circumstances are different. You know," he said, cocking his finger, "bang bang."

18

Later that night as they lay entangled, Patricia wryly observed that Rowe wasn't always gentle with her during sex. To his surprise, she informed him quietly that he could be even rougher with her if he liked. He propped himself on an elbow and looked at her. Her make-up had faded and there was a faint glow of perspiration.

"Are you into that sort of thing?"

"Well . . ." She stroked her damp hair. "I was involved with a couple in the S and M community for a while, but I broke it off."

"Why?"

"They'd gone against the code. There's an unwritten code that the sub's always the person with the most power, because the sub has the right to stop what's happening at any time. They control the energy."

"By 'sub' you mean submissive. It was a bisexual triangle then?"

Patricia looked guarded as she started to reach for the sheet, but seemed to relax. "The woman was a bisexual, but I'm not. She did some things to me, but I didn't do anything to her."

Her breasts sagged slightly and were uneven in size; she'd told him that the smaller of the two was scarred from the removal of a benign cyst. There were stretch marks across her midsection. Her narrow waist broadened at her hips and heavier thighs, where her pubic hair formed a reddish-brown V.

"What were they like?"

"Well, he was forty-nine, and had a shaved head and a lot of tattoos. She was forty-one. The last time we were together he wouldn't stop when I asked him to. They were quite insulting to me when I left."

"What was he doing to you, exactly?"

"I can't tell you those kinds of details. If you were experienced or had that sensibility, you'd know."

Rowe was bothered by her vaguely dismissive tone. As he stroked her arm, he said, "Whips, candle wax? What did they force up your pretty ass?"

"I don't like it when you swear."

"Sorry. You hang out with punks and sadists but don't like swearing." Rowe moved his hand over her scalp and gripped her by the hair, slowly pulling her head back. "Did you get fisted?"

"No," she answered mildly, "but I have put the necks of wine bottles up my bum. And you apologize too much."

He released her. "You put them up there yourself?"

"Masturbation is always more satisfying than intercourse."

"Not to me."

"Of course; it's common knowledge. Only you know exactly what you want."

Rowe attempted to unpeel some tissue he'd used to clean himself. "For me it's a last resort. Men will go through fire to be with a woman."

"Come on. Men will always masturbate. Even if they're in a relationship they'll still keep up their usual pattern. It's their nature."

"I don't even like it much when I don't have a girlfriend. It's depressing and reminds me that I'm lonely."

"Well, you're unique then. I have a friend who masturbates eighteen times a day."

Rowe was getting annoyed by her contrary edge. He abandoned the tissue. "A man can't even *come* eighteen times a day."

"Well, maybe he doesn't always do it that much, but I know he has. I've had sex seven times with someone in one night. But anyway, masturbation is still better." With a smug smile she added primly, "I've even knit a hat for my dildo."

"I'm glad that works for you," he said, lying back. "As far as I'm concerned, there's no substitute for real contact."

"You sound obsessed. I'd rather have a good meal any day."

Rowe felt he was losing ground in an absurd debate. "Well, you must have thought it was important enough to have become so good at oral sex."

Patricia looked pleased by the compliment. "I just wish I could get more of your cock in my mouth."

"I also like how you can put your ankles on either side of your head."

She sniffed. "All women can do that."

"Well, no," Rowe said, "they can't."

He looked away. Dresses were hanging inside the open door of an old wardrobe in the corner. Clothes had been flung over the back of a chair. A sense of disorder existed on the top of her dresser in a kind of mix-and-match feminine bohemia: combs and brushes and cosmetics, candles, an incense dish, one old doll sitting splay-legged in a blue and white dress. It seemed an architectural oddity that the entrance to their main floor and basement was at the back of the house, while her bedroom window faced the front porch.

"Is your friend Jack seeing anybody?" she asked.

"A black stripper. At least as far as I know they're still going out."

"Why did you say 'black'?"

"She's black."

Patricia's smile was grim. There was an apologetic note in her voice, but she seemed subtly determined. "I don't know why you have to say she's 'black', as if that's important in how you define her."

Rowe sighed. "It's not a put-down; I'm just describing her. You don't see a lot of white guys with black girls. It's usually the other way around."

"I don't know what you're saying, really," she said quietly. "The same number of white men go out with black women as black men go out with white women. Just about all of my male friends have had black girlfriends at one time or another."

Maybe this gentle provocation was calculated to lure him into giving her the back of his hand. She might be testing him to see if he had the mettle. He didn't like the idea of her deliberately playing him, so it was probably working. "It's common knowledge, it's a fucking *cliché*—black men chasing white women. Anyway," he said impatiently, "why did you want to know about Jack?"

"I was just thinking about Maggie," she said, repositioning herself. "She's sworn off men. Not officially, but she hasn't had sex in three years."

"What's her problem?"

"She has high standards. She finds something wrong with everyone." Patricia checked her tissue and reached for the box of Kleenex. "You came too much, I think. You always come a lot, don't you?"

"Sure, the chicks love me because I'm a stud."

"They love you for *this*? I don't think so. No woman likes to clean up a mess, believe me. And I don't know why you're stoned so much when you have sex," she added benignly. "Marijuana just makes me frigid."

Rowe didn't like hearing these kinds of things; they gave him the sense that he'd had everything all wrong, all along. Every time he turned around now, it seemed as if some woman was trying to tell him that his semen was a disgrace or that he'd fucked his life away.

"Mind if I get a beer?" he asked, getting off the bed. "You probably think I drink too much, too."

"Not compared to my ex-husband."

"Do you want one?"

"No, I'm going to go to sleep soon. And you know I can't really afford to buy beer."

"I'll bring some next time."

He walked through the living room on his way to the kitchen, and noticed a couple of Yardbirds and Ramones CDs on her coffee table. When he returned, Patricia was lying on her side. Oddly, as with his changing impression of her in the bar, he thought he perceived a kind of old style Hollywood thing in the pale eyes and the sheen of her full-bodied hair beneath the bulb. She definitely looked better without the glasses. He sat back down on the bed next to her, and took a pull on the bottle. "So your husband liked to drink."

"When he was in the band he was out of control." She slowly shifted up onto her elbow. "I was very surprised to find out he was cheating on me when they were on the road."

"I guess that's pretty common with musicians."

"Not with him. He was in love with me." Patricia seemed to sense his skepticism. "When I was sick for two years and we couldn't have sex, I know for a fact that he never cheated on me or even masturbated."

"Sick with what?"

"Mono. My health has never been very good. I've got asthma and have had bronchitis, shingles, infections. . . . Anyway," she said solemnly, "if you're in a relationship—"

"Sorry, but how would you know if he masturbated?"

"I just know him. If you're in a relationship for a long time, you realize that sex isn't that important because you've reached a deeper level with one another. You're on a higher plane."

"There are a lot of married people out there who can't be bothered having sex any more, and I don't think that puts them on a higher plane," he said.

"You're very cynical and negative. I prefer people who are more positive."

"Punks and sadists."

Afterwards, they went downstairs to the bathroom in her basement. The space was small, and the ceiling slanted. Rowe leaned against the sink and washed himself while Patricia sat down to pee. "I'm going to get fat," she stated. "I'm just going to let it happen, and be one of those women who wears her pants up around her chest."

Even her complacency was annoying him. Rowe cupped a hand under his testicles to prevent water running off onto the floor.

As Patricia flushed the toilet, it was clear that her unpleasant smile was intended to offset another rude reality. "I hope you're not the stalking type," she said. "After we break up, you're not going to try to get back together by calling all the time, are you? I don't find that kind of thing very attractive."

"No, baby," he said, "that's not my style." The weight of her words hung in the air as Rowe heard the kiss-off. He didn't know if spontaneity counted for anything in sadomasochism, and tried to keep his expression neutral as he grabbed her by the hair, tilting back her head to press a kiss on her as he manhandled her tits, twisting the nipples.

"What are you *doing*?" she said, struggling while he forced her to her knees, then worked her onto all fours with her face dangerously close to the toilet bowl.

"Disciplining you." Rowe pushed her thighs apart with his leg as he got a better grip on her tresses, and spanked her while she thrashed and shouted. Holding her with one arm around her hip, he cupped her crotch and probed her lips for the opening while trying to manipulate her clit.

Wrestling her back into position as Patricia fought to twist free, Rowe intermittently smacked her ass while he got his knees between hers, managing to force her thighs apart and lubricate himself as he worked his prick against her. During a lapse in her resistance he pulled one of her cheeks wide to see her asshole above the progress of his penetration, her hair wrapped around his fist, and heard her grunt when he began to fuck her. She was a big girl. If this shit didn't earn some respect from her, at least it would give him some peace of mind.

19

Robert O'Hara went home after The Black Bull to pick up more coke for a warehouse rave, where he'd catch up with Kim and Betty. When he rounded the back corner of his house he didn't notice the men in the darkness until he was turning the key in his lock and they charged down the steps behind him, shoving him into the hallway. He tripped onto one knee, trying to grab the wall, when a pipe cracked him across his head and split his scalp. Someone's boot caught him in the ribs as he hit the wooden floor. While he attempted to roll away and get to his feet, he went sideways into the plaster, his hair in his eyes, and kept moving.

"You're dead meat, fucker," the one named Vince said, pulling a knife from his fringed jacket. His face flash-framed under the light as O'Hara warded off another blow from the pipe while trying to run for the kitchen. He was tackled in the tiny living room by the big one, Frank, who kept bringing his elbow down on him from behind until O'Hara struggled into another position, randomly connecting with wild swings until the pipe dropped onto the floor and he was held more tightly with a forearm across his neck. While he was beaten and kicked, his nose was broken.

He was blinded by pain but remembered while he was yelling that the people upstairs were away. "What do you *want?*" He was hardly aware of his tears as he swallowed blood.

Frank breathed alcohol into his face as he pinned him down on his back. "Two fucking grand." Hawking up some saliva, he slowly spit as O'Hara tried to turn away.

"I'm gonna cut him." Vince came close with his knife out. He lay the blade along O'Hara's cheek and pressed the point into the flesh, drawing downwards. Blood welled from the slice.

"Stop! Please, fuck—*stop*! I'll give you the money!"

"Of course you will, asshole." Frank stared down at him with bleary eyes. "But we're going to fuck you up anyway."

Vince gripped O'Hara's hair and managed to force the blade down his other cheek while he was bucking and pleading. "If I go there will be trouble; if I stay it will be . . ."

O'Hara's face was slick with blood and spit. His nose was disfigured and one eye already felt as if it was swelling. He probed a loose tooth with his tongue. Vince wiped the knife on O'Hara's forehead, and stood up, kicking him in the side. "Wanna do him like we did Huey?" he asked, putting his foot on Robert.

"What do you fucking *want*? I'll give you the coke. Money too."

"Oh, so you *are* in the business," Vince said. "Hear that, man? He *is* still in the business after telling us he wasn't."

"I'm not. I just do blow myself, now."

"Now he says he wants to blow us."

Frank laughed. "Well, maybe we'll let him before we fuck him up, *if* he gives us everything." He drew his fist back. "How much do you have? You got two fucking thousand and lots of coke?" He lightly pressed his thumb on the bridge of Robert's nose.

O'Hara screamed, struggling under the man's weight. "Yeah, yeah, *stop*! Stop—*please*!"

Vince squatted and held the blade to his throat. "Fuck, let's just kill him."

Frank seemed to smile. "I don't know. . . . How much money you got, fucker?"

O'Hara was blubbering. "Fifteen hundred, but I can get more."

"And how much coke's in the house?"

He swallowed. "Few grams, that's all."

"And you got all that right here. Fifteen hundred."

"Yeah."

"You better not be bullshitting us," Frank said, slowly getting off him. His hands, sleeves and the front of his shirt were bloody. He reached for the pipe. "Where is it?"

O'Hara touched his wet face lightly. He hurt everywhere, and thought a couple of ribs might be cracked. Vince held the knife as he watched him rise, and said, "You heard him. Where the fuck is it?"

"I've got it stashed." He rose awkwardly and walked slowly into the kitchen with the two men behind him. Crouching, O'Hara felt around in the cupboard under the sink among the cleansers for one of the guns. He touched the Ruger's cylinder and checked the safety as he handled the rubber grip, knowing a bullet was in the chamber, and fired upwards at the closest one as he turned on his haunches. Frank, hit in the stomach, fell backwards over a chair. Vince stood transfixed for a second before he bolted, but O'Hara shot him in the back. He collided with the door jamb as he went down.

Frank was moaning. O'Hara walked over and aimed at his head as he squeezed off another round. There was some blow-back. He stood on quaking legs, taking in the dead eyes and what he guessed was brain and bone matter, before throwing up onto the dirty tile. After a couple of steps he felt dizzy and lost consciousness.

When O'Hara came to he was lying in blood and vomit. He got up and looked around, touching his face. He wanted to do a line to alleviate the pain, but breathing through his nose was an ordeal. He went to the washroom to check the extent of the damage and could see that the lacerations were going to scar if he didn't get to a hospital, where he'd have to have his nose reset, his head stitched or stapled, and he might even need plastic surgery. He started to wash the blood from his face and matted hair, but stopped, wondering if he should keep it like that for the police, or get somebody to take a photo of him.

One of them had been shot in the back, though, and the second bullet in the other guy would be hard to explain too. Plus, the Ruger linked him to the bank. O'Hara paced the house as the impossibility of the situation sunk in. What if he said he'd somehow shot them with their own gun? He'd have to get one of their fingerprints on it. . . . Would he have to confess to the coke thing to make it more believable? That is, after he flushed everything in the house down the toilet.

O'Hara got a beer from the refrigerator and walked back into the bathroom, where he stanched the blood and tried to seal the slashes with Band-Aids and toilet paper. He had to pause to wipe away tears.

After wandering around, he picked up the phone but replaced the receiver. He looked too ruined to go find Kim or even Betty to help him figure it out. Maybe he'd have to take his chances with the police after going to the hospital. Call his mother to hire a lawyer. Get somebody to take that photo. But first he'd have to think through the part about it being their gun, and why he'd shot one guy at close range who was already down, what they might call execution-style, and the other in the back. Maybe he'd have to call Derek, but he'd be so fucking pissed off about the gun and everything. There hadn't been time to worry about it when he'd been rooting around under the sink.

O'Hara finished off his beer as he walked around, tracking blood, trying to get it together. It was ten after one. He might have to use the other number Derek had given him for emergencies if he wasn't at home. While he was in the kitchen opening another beer, he jumped at a barely perceptible groan from Vince on the floor. Grabbing a steak knife from the dish rack, he stabbed him in the back and left the blade in him. Now the prick was dead.

20

After leaving Rowe and his girlfriend at the Bull, Lofton decided to take the subway to Parkdale to catch up with Marva following her shift at the bar.

He was sitting on the edge of her bathtub while she wiped her face with a washcloth, admiring the integrity of those breasts which culminated in two dark, protuberant nipples. There was a red heart on the crotch of her panties. It occurred to him that without her make-up her face exuded the kind of neutrality that could have easily belonged to a church volunteer or hotel maid. It was certainly better that she was a stripper. Her lack of sophistication was becoming less important with each passing day.

"We ought to go to Montana's sometime," she said.

"I hate line-ups. I won't go anywhere there's a line-up."

"I don't mind waiting, because if you get there too early you look like the welcoming committee. I usually go around ten when it's just starting. It doesn't take very long." Marva walked to the doorway, pausing as he got up, and said, "I don't think the bouncers at Montana's like me very much. I had a birthday party there last year and reserved one of the rooms, but they gave it away before I got there—even though I was only *fifteen* minutes late."

They crossed the hall. Pushing aside the sheet, she said, "I asked them if they were prejudiced, and they didn't like that."

"They can't keep a room reserved if nobody shows up."

"I was going there all the time. They knew I was a good customer."

"Look," he said, climbing onto the bed, "you're on the pill so we don't have to use rubbers anymore, right? You know I can't really feel anything."

"You've got to get tested. Go to the doctor."

He sighed. "I won't come inside you."

"No, you can still get AIDS that way." Marva watched him pull his shirt over his head, then leaned back and raised her bum to wriggle out of her panties. "You're very gentlemanly when you have sex, aren't you? You look so big and bad, but like we hardly even break into a sweat or anything."

He squinted at her. "You don't know how lucky you are. You wouldn't like my dark side, *believe* me."

As she was looking back at him, the telephone rang. Lofton tensed. The chance he was taking by being there was ridiculously apparent. He sucked his teeth in elaborate disgust as he looked up at the ceiling. "Don't answer; it might be that asshole again."

"Maybe it's important." Marva turned over and picked up the receiver. "Hello?" There was an actual expression of surprise on her face. "Oh . . . hi. That's okay . . . Yeah, he's here; just a minute." She held out the phone. "It's for you. Your friend Derek."

As Lofton took it, she ducked under the twisted cord and moved away while he rolled over. "Hello? Yeah, hi, what's going on?" He frowned, listening. "What? Are you kidding? Holy shit . . . Tell me exactly—oh, man, I don't fucking *believe* this."

When he hung up, Lofton reached for his beer and wondered how much he could tell her. He took a pull and said, "I have to go out. It's an emergency. I can't go into the details, but there's been a shooting involving a friend of ours."

"Who? How come you have to go? How did he have my number?"

"I gave it to him in case he needed to reach me for something important. He's picking me up. He couldn't go into too much about it over the phone, but we have to go see this guy because my expertise is needed."

"Is he in the hospital?"

"I don't think so," he said, getting off the bed, "but it's serious and it looks like they may need my assistance with an investigation. The police are going to be involved, and they'll want my input." He gave her a significant look. "I'll check things out and tell them *only* what they need to know."

He thought he caught her glancing at his grey T-shirt as he pulled it on, either at the half-dried sweat stains or at the faded writing that said WITNESS RELOCATION PROGRAM, and wondering if it was serious.

Marva reached for her panties and asked, "Well, are you coming back?"

"I don't know." He straightened his bandanna as he looked around for his socks. "Probably."

"Well, I'm going to sleep, so if you're coming back you should knock loud so I wake up. It's after two. I don't know how you're going to have time." Marva got off the bed. She pulled out a dresser drawer and picked through some lingerie. Pulling out a pink nightie, she asked, "And what's with all these guns? You've got friends in shootings in the middle of the night. This is like living with Tyrone."

Lofton didn't mind the analogy. Trying to remember what he'd told her as he lit a cigarette, he said, "I explained I do PI work. I'm licensed to carry a gun. The guy we're going to see is in security."

As he pushed the sheet aside and went into the washroom, he tried to piece together the details Rowe had given him. The only thing that was clear was that the shit was hitting the fan.

Twenty minutes later, Lofton was climbing into the Firebird. "So, let me get this straight," he said. "Robert actually killed those guys with one of our guns, and he's still got the bodies in his fucking *house*?"

Rowe put his cigarette in the ashtray. "Looks like it. Leave your beer outside the car."

"Fuck, that's the last thing you've got to be worrying about."

"Just leave it. We've got enough problems."

He sighed as he upended the bottle for a final swallow. When he opened the door and put it on the sidewalk, it fell with a hollow clink, and rolled. The night was quiet. Lofton could almost see the humour in the situation, but Rowe looked grim as he pulled away from the curb.

Lofton pushed in the lighter on the dashboard, and took out his Camels. "I told you he was a fucking moron. You know what we've got to do, don't you?"

"What?"

"We've got to shoot Robert with the Beretta."

Rowe smiled tiredly as he put on his indicator and slowed down at King. He checked traffic but didn't come to a full stop before turning east.

"*Think* about it. You've got the murder weapons from the bank, plus what'll look like three dead bank robbers. Some of the money will be there too. Get their prints on everything. Case closed. Maybe there was some kind of Mexican standoff. But even if that doesn't add up, it doesn't fucking matter; the cops are still going to have the three guys they're looking for. Maybe there was a drug war or something. They're not really going to give a shit."

As they drove past the string of bars and closed restaurants at Dufferin, Lofton looked at the people in the vicinity of the intersection. There was the odd homeless person, what looked like a hooker, and a few brothers in touques and hoods. A police cruiser was parked in the McDonald's lot.

"The Beretta's still in the ravine," Rowe said. "There's no way I could find it in the dark."

Lofton didn't think he'd been paying attention. He smoked as he looked down the dark streets of warehouses and

factories to the south, before they drove under the railway trestle. There was a stadium, a Chrysler Dodge Jeep dealership,
open land, boarded-up buildings. He tapped his cigarette on
the ashtray, trying to think it through. "So we go and pretend
to clean up a bit, get hold of the Glock or Ruger . . . It'd be
better if the Beretta was there, too; maybe we can find it when
the sun comes up. You said that chick of his doesn't live there,
so he'll be alone."

"Aside from the fact that I don't want to be shooting
Robert," Rowe said, "there are too many loose ends. Times of
death might be close enough, but neighbours will start coming out of the woodwork, saying how they heard what they
later realized were shots, but at different times. Or if they did-
n't hear the first ones, maybe they'll hear the next one, and
we'll still have cops at the door. It'd be too risky to go back to
the house in the daylight even if I found the gun. Also, we
don't know if he's spoken to those friends of his, who'll probably say that we were involved with him. I told him not talk to
anyone, but he's flipping out. Or those people will just go over
there anyway, looking for coke or whatever."

"Just think about it," Lofton said. "We'll see how it looks
when we get there."

"Forensics will check powder burns, angles of entry, anything inconsistent with . . ." Rowe seemed to be talking to
himself as he lowered his window.

Lofton considered it. There was a good plan in there
somewhere, one that might give them Robert's share of the
take, whatever coke was lying around, and clear them of the
robbery at the same time.

They passed an old hotel, lofts and townhouses under construction, a donut shop, market, lighting and electrical supply
company, old buildings. Rowe turned left at Niagara, north to
Queen, and headed east another two blocks. As they drove up
Euclid, everything was silent and deserted. Leaves were blowing across the street. There didn't appear to be any police cars

around, marked or unmarked, when they slowly passed a semi-detached house with ivy, trees, bushes, and a small porch with a wrought iron railing. It was dark except for a light over the front door.

"Sure you got the right address?"

"He's around the back. Nobody else is home."

"I think it's parking-by-permit at now," Lofton said. "We don't want to get placed at the scene by a ticket."

Rowe put the car in reverse and began backing into a space. "That's a chance we're going to have to take."

Lofton glanced around as they got out. He took a last drag, and stepped on his butt before following Rowe along the sidewalk and down a pathway at the side of the house. Around the corner, a light was burning by the screen door at the bottom of some cement steps.

When O'Hara opened the door, he looked like he'd gone through a windshield. His hair was drenched with blood from what seemed the crown of his head, and had soaked through bandages on either side of his face. He might have been crying. His face looked puffy, out of alignment.

"Christ," Rowe said.

Holding some stained toilet paper to his nose, O'Hara took a drink of beer as they walked past him, and closed the door. "I've gotta go to a hospital."

"What'd they want?" Lofton asked.

"Money, coke, to kill me—I don't know. They were fucking nuts."

The three men walked through a hallway to a tiny living room with white plaster walls, shabby furniture, and a ghetto blaster with detachable speakers on a side table. A lamp had been knocked over, and there was blood on the rumpled rug.

"You didn't call anybody else, right?" Lofton said.

"No."

He surveyed the surroundings. Rowe was too close to the situation to make an intelligent assessment. Lofton squeezed past him in a doorway to see a man lying twisted in a pool of blood on the kitchen floor, with a knife in his back.

Rowe followed him in as he stepped over the body. The black and white tile was smeared red, and the place smelled like puke. Chairs were overturned, and there was a big moth-erfucker on the floor who looked gut-shot and had a hole in his head. The wall and floor behind him were as sprayed and clotted as an abstract painting. Lofton hadn't expected this from O'Hara, and was reluctantly impressed. It cancelled the standoff scenario, however. "You got another beer there, Capone?"

"Give me one too," Rowe said, crouching by the heavy one.

O'Hara's face looked bad, and his tangled hair was stuck together. He pulled out a bottle and passed it back. "So, what do you think?"

"Well, they seem pretty dead," Lofton said, twisting off the cap.

Rowe took a beer and walked over to crouch beside the guy close to the doorway. "First, you're going to have to tell your old man that two of his guns were stolen. And you've got to—" His fingers were pressed to the man's neck. "Fuck, this one's still alive."

"*What*?" O'Hara's mouth was open. "I don't believe—"

Lofton put his bottle on the counter and lit another smoke. Snapping his lighter shut, he said, "All right. Give me your gun."

Rowe didn't move.

"This dick's a witness to everything: Murder Two during some kind of drug thing, with a gun that was also used to kill someone during the commission of a felony that ties you and me into it. You want to go to prison for twenty years?"

"I didn't kill anyone," Rowe said.

"Oh, is that how it is? I had to *save* you. And you're still an accessory to murder, and an armed bank robber."

"I know what the fuck I am. Don't be giving orders."

Lofton picked up his bottle and took a drink. "Well, you know what we've got to do." He sensed Rowe had blinked, and he was now in charge. "Robert, where's the gun? You got a pillow or anything?"

Rowe was silent as O'Hara took the Ruger from the cutlery drawer and handed it to Lofton, then went into the other room and came back with a sofa cushion. The others stepped back as Lofton approached the unconscious man. Despite his pounding heart, he looked calm. With the cigarette in his mouth, he placed the cushion against the back of the man's head, and was raising the barrel when his arm was grabbed.

"Wait," Rowe said. He pulled the knife out as he turned the man over, and took the cushion from Lofton. He put it over the upturned face and leaned down to put some weight into it. O'Hara wiped away some hair, and slowly righted a chair to sit down. After a moment, Rowe examined the body. "We didn't want any more noise. And you're positive nobody's home."

O'Hara, gingerly touching his nose with index finger and thumb, turned from the corpse to look at him. "Yeah. How am I ever going to clean all this shit?"

Lofton picked up his beer and left to find a washroom. There was a trail of blood in the hallway, more around the sink and toilet, even drops on the roll of paper. The place looked like a slaughterhouse.

When he walked back out, they were laying the stained living room rug in the hallway outside the kitchen. Rowe nudged it straight with his boot, and said to him, "Let's carry the big one out first."

Lofton stepped around the first body and put his bottle on the counter. With one last drag, he laid his cigarette along the sink before turning and slipping on some vomit. He went down with a crash. He swore as he raised himself onto an elbow, before Rowe put a hand under his arm to help him up. Lofton looked himself over. There was puke and blood on his leather jacket, his hip and the side of his bad leg. "Fuck!"

Rowe reached for some paper towels. "We don't want that crap in the car."

After that they lifted the first man by his arms and legs and lugged him from the kitchen. Lofton and Rowe rolled him up in the rug, and with O'Hara supporting the middle, carried him outside and along the house to the street. Lofton watched the neighbouring windows while Rowe unlocked the trunk.

Back in the house, O'Hara changed his bandages. There was seepage from his earlier scalp injury. They sliced through the bottom of some green garbage bags and pulled them over the midsection of the other body, taping them together, and put two more over his head, feet and legs, and secured them with string.

"I don't know if they can dust for prints off this plastic," Lofton said.

"We should wipe it."

They'd already handled the other sides of the bags, but Lofton didn't want to start over. "We ought to be wearing those dish gloves."

"Look," O'Hara said, "I've really got to go to the hospital to get my nose fixed, and get some Demerol or morphine or something."

Rowe stood up. "Later. Give me the roll of towels. Jack, we should wipe off whatever we've touched around here. We can clean the bags when we're dumping them. Robert, don't forget to pick up the casings and wipe them before you throw them out, somewhere far away from here." He took a drink. "You have to seriously clean this up before you go to the hospital, in case the police want to talk to you. You've got Mr. Clean or something?"

"I can't do all that shit now," O'Hara said, touching his face again. "Aren't you two going to help clean this? I'm in bad shape."

"We have to move your boyfriends the fuck *out* of here," Lofton said. "And you better wash this place enough for the cops in the fucking space suits looking for DNA."

"Another couple of hours aren't going to kill you," Rowe added. "We'll come back later with some bleach or something. Get a mop; don't wait for the blood to dry. Our footprints are on the floor, so we might have to get rid of our shoes if we leave tracks outside." He picked up the Ruger. "And I need this too."

"I can't—"

"The fucking Glock too; there were casings on the floor of the bank. Tell your old man that the guns were stolen, because we're clearing everything out of here. And the ammunition. Don't tell Betty or anyone about any of this, even a year from now." He looked the room over as he finished off the bottle. "The cops won't need bodies, just forensic evidence. We'll be back in a while to go over it a second time. "

O'Hara gathered his hair behind his head, as if to wring it out. "Where you going to dump them?"

"I don't know yet. Listen, give me a blanket. This guy's probably got to go on the back floor."

21

When Lofton left her apartment, Marva Johnson called Jacqueline. The sister usually went out clubbing after her shift at Burger King and stayed up late, especially since her kids had been put into foster care. She said she and her boyfriend and another girl from the Jane-Finch corridor had been at the Bamboo to see the Reggae Cowboys. Marva could hear them laughing in the background as she told her about Jack's friend getting shot. When Jacqueline asked her how, and by who, she pulled her nightie out from under her and rolled onto her back. "I don't know. I asked him but he wouldn't tell me any details. His friend came and got him, and he just left."

"Hey," Jacqueline shouted, half-muffled, "I can't *hear.* So what are you gonna do? That sounds fucked up."

"Tell me about it."

"You've had the worst luck with men."

Marva drank some water. "He's all right. I just don't know what's going on right now."

"So is he coming back, or what? Tonight, I mean."

"I think so. Oh—I didn't tell you who I saw yesterday." She turned onto her stomach and propped herself on both elbows. "You'll never guess."

"Who?"

"You know the guy in the movie *RoboCop*? I don't remember his name, but the robocop."

"Where—in the bar where you dance?"

Marva laughed. "No, in a shoe store on Bloor, near Yorkville. He saw me looking at him, trying to figure out if it was him or not, and he turns and says, 'Yeah, it's me.' He was acting cool. He must be up here making another movie."

"What'd you say?"

"I just said, 'Oh, yeah, it is.' He looked busy, so I didn't really try to talk or anything."

After she hung up, Marva used the toilet and thought about calling somebody else, but decided to watch TV. She walked back out to the living room and sat on the sofa, flipping past infomercials about hair weaves and acne cures before she found a movie, but it was an old musical with white people in tuxedos and shit. After that she landed on a flick with Tupac Shakur and Samuel Jackson, which she remembered had Tupac tripping out on his friends, with Jackson in the background as some kind of older influence before he got really big.

Marva was about to go to bed when there was a knock on the door. It was too dark to see anybody on the driveway through the half-drawn curtains. She flipped the latch and turned the handle.

Tyrone was standing there with Rasheed and Ice up on the steps behind him. "How you doin'?" he asked, deadpan as he looked past her, a hand inside his coat. Before she could say anything, he was coming in.

"Hey," she said, "wait!"

The others pushed past her, Rasheed last. "What up?"

Tyrone walked through the living room with his gun drawn, and checked out the bathroom and kitchenette, then pushed aside the sheet to her bedroom. "Your white-ass boyfriend ain't here no more?" At the end of the hallway he opened the door to Tony's room and looked in. "Whose shit is this?"

"My roommate," she said, going into her bedroom for a housecoat. "What do you want?"

When she came back out, Ice was in the kitchen looking in the refrigerator, his gun on the counter. His sunglasses were hooked over his ears in reverse, as if the back of his bowling ball head was a face. He was big and looked uglier than the last time she'd seen him, wearing his designer jeans low and baggy, half off his ass, a red nylon jacket over a black sweatshirt.

"You trying to find something?"

He glanced back at her but didn't say anything.

"Who's this roommate you got here, living in my space?" Tyrone walked out to the living room ahead of her with his gun shoulder-holstered, and stopped in front of the TV. "Hey, my *man*—Tupac. What the fuck is this?"

"That one where he an' this other brother are gunning for each other," Rasheed said, throwing out an arm in a downward swing. "You know, man, where Tupac's a wild motherfucker, killing other homeys and shit, and fucking somebody up for leadership."

Marva thought he was one of the better friends, even if he was a bit loud, but he had what looked like a submachine gun in his lap as he sat with his legs outstretched, rangy body twist-ed on the sofa, pumped-up Converse hi-tops on the coffee table. He was wearing his black touque pulled down, marked X, and his jacket collar turned up. The stubble around his heavy lips looked like the beginning of a goatee.

"What are you guys doing here?" she demanded.

"Who's this roommate? I'm asking you *again*, girl," Tyrone said, looking at her. He had a faint smirk so she'd know he was being mellow and not get pissed, but he wasn't prepared to be ignored in front of his boys. His hair was in corn rows and he had a diamond stud in his left ear lobe, a couple of gold chains around his neck. Classier than when he was wearing that clock-on-a-rope thing like Flavor Flav. Even with the gap between his front teeth, he figured his good looks made him God's Gift.

"And I *told* you—a roommate's a roommate. A guy who moved in here to help pay the rent. I hardly see him; he works nights." Marva pulled her housecoat tighter. "It's almost three in the morning. What are you doing with those guns? Are you stoned or something?"

Tyrone went back to looking at the TV, then picked up a framed photo of her in hot pants and put it back down. "We're going to make you a proposition. We want to bring some stuff over for you to keep, awright? Some merchandise nobody's going to be looking for here. We gonna cut you in, so you be happy too." It wasn't a question. Being a natural-born hustler, he always adapted his way of talking to the situation. When he was explaining their fight to the police, it came off like he was a high school graduate and she was a crack whore. Everybody was a potential mark he had to con or intimidate.

"What—drugs?"

"Maybe some of that. I know you not stupid enough to do that shit, so I can trust you around it. Also, maybe some other things like car radios, CD players, DVDs, computer parts, shit like that."

"A few guns too," Ice said behind her.

Tyrone frowned at him. "Well, we see how this goes first. This roommate and that punk-ass boyfriend of yours—they both boning you, or what?"

Marva stepped clear of them. "What?"

"You doin' the wild thing," Rasheed explained. He aimed his gun at the TV and pretended to spray the screen.

"I don't give a fuck," Tyrone clarified, cool and reasonable. "What I want to know is, you can hide shit and trust them to stay out of it?"

"My roommate doesn't know what I do," she said, "but my boyfriend's still around, and he'll be pissed off if he finds you guys here. He's not going to like you keeping anything here, either. You *know* he's got a gun too."

"That don't mean shit." Tyrone put a hand to the side of his head, checking the weaves while he thought about it, then put his face up to Marva's. "We gonna stick to the plan, and if you know what's good, bitch, you gonna help us out, if'n you don't want your boyfriend dead. I don't care if he's got a fuckin' bazooka; he won't know what's gonna come down, *when* it's gonna come down. And you might get capped too if everybody's emotional, you know what I'm saying?" He stepped back. "You be cool, and we be good to you, awright? You'll make some cash, and we'll take care of you. And you won't have to worry about anybody's ass getting shot. All you gotta do is make sure you're alone when we come back, and mind some stuff for us. Keep him and the fuckin' roommate out of it."

She stood there with her arms folded, not saying anything.

"We might be back, or I'll call you when we're ready. Be cool."

Tyrone jerked his head. Rasheed got off the sofa, and the three of them took their time walking out the door.

22

Rowe took Lake Shore Boulevard east past Parliament and turned right on Cherry, which ran south to the tip of the jutting shoreline. It was a wide street, nearly deserted at that hour, with low buildings and industrial yards. They drove over a bridge and passed a hydroelectric facility with huge tanks behind a fence warning of guard dogs. Then an isolated restaurant. East down Commissioners a towering smokestack was visible near Carlaw, its lights blinking against a dark sky and grey clouds. Maybe the same chimney that he'd noticed from the bridge over the ravine up on St. Clair.

Despite the current crisis, Patricia remained in the back of his mind. Increasingly, she'd been quietly arguing with almost everything he said, but seemed strangely quiet after he'd administered what would have been the fatal blow to any other relationship. She'd still got in the last word there too, when he faked a hint of regret in her bathroom to circumvent a possible rape charge, and had been told again with what might have been condescension that he apologized too much. At least now he had a better idea of what she expected, anyway.

They passed a vast wholesale supermarket called Knob Hill Farms, and then the grounds of The Docks, a nightclub and entertainment complex to the west on Polson. Lofton asked him if he'd ever been inside. Rowe glanced past the fenced-in netting that contained what looked like a driving range, to the buildings on the edge of the harbour. He said no.

"Says they've got a swimming pool and golf."

"I've never golfed in my life."

"I'm a good golfer," Lofton said, looking out the window.

"Fuck off." Rowe glanced at him. "When have you ever golfed?"

"I used to golf all the fuckin' time in L.A."

The Firebird rumbled over a drawbridge. On their left, a small building near the edge of the canal housed boats under repair. To the right was Lake Ontario, where anchored freighters, tugboats and other ships were dimly visible in the harbour between Centre Island and the downtown waterfront. Beyond the docked ferries lights shone from the windows of office buildings in a skyline made distinct by the CN Tower and the SkyDome arena, which was bathed in a mauve glow.

They drove by a towing yard and office trailer, where a sign was posted on a double fence topped by barbed wire to keep out intruders. After that, a self-storage warehouse, equipment rentals, and a street to the east that seemingly led to another huge smokestack. Straight ahead, past some small buildings that might have been change houses or snack concessions, the beach was nothing but darkness.

Lofton's face appeared in an orange glow as he flicked his lighter. Exhaling, he asked if this was the place. Rowe said it was.

"You just want to dump them in there?"

"It's wilder past the trees to the right, where there's more weeds and shit. Over there they might not get found right away."

"There are probably bodies in there already."

Above the road a sign said Clarke Beach. They drove slowly into the dirt parking lot. When Rowe turned to the right, his heart lurched as the Firebird's headlights swept across a white police cruiser parked by the side. "Fucking hell—"

"Get the fuck out of here."

Rowe felt short of breath as he made an unhurried U-turn and glanced in the rearview mirror as the cop car disappeared into darkness, half-expecting to see the panel of lights, or hear a siren whoop. Carefully, he stepped on the accelerator as they drove back out onto Cherry Street, wondering if he should boot it for the Gardiner Expressway.

Lofton looked back. "Good choice."

"Maybe he's busy with a hooker."

As they crossed the small bridge, Rowe slowed down enough to take the Ruger from his coat and wipe it off with his shirt. He was putting it into the glove compartment with the barrel in the crook of his hand when Lofton shouted, and he swerved back from the curb. The knife, which he'd already wiped, was wrapped up in his other pocket. As he glanced in the mirror again he saw the squad car emerge from the parking lot behind them. "Christ."

With the cigarette in his mouth, Lofton looked out the back window and adjusted the blanket on the corpse. "Go faster."

"He's not pulling us over," Rowe said, checking the mirror. "I don't want to look like I'm trying to outrun him." The cruiser was gaining ground.

"Faster. Fucking step on it!"

"He's not after us," Rowe said, "but wipe off the Glock." He inadvertently crossed the meridian as he looked back at the blanket, and was up to 60 KPH when they heard the siren. The cruiser was behind him with its lights flashing. He slowed to turn right on Commissioners, uncertain whether to make a break for it, and kept his speed steady.

"What the fuck are you *doing*?" Lofton shouted.

"There isn't enough traffic. We wouldn't be able to lose him."

"Fuck!"

Rowe sped up, then lost his nerve and put on his turn signal. He couldn't concentrate. "There aren't any warrants," he said, trying to talk above Lofton, "and I'm not going to blow over. It's just a traffic thing. He's already got the fucking plate number."

Lofton put his cigarette in the ashtray and opened the glove compartment.

Rowe saw the officer get out of the cruiser in his rearview mirror. The police radio was audible as the red and whites revolved in the empty street. "Put that away," he said, grabbing Lofton's arm as he was checking the Ruger's cylinder for bullets.

They struggled over the revolver and broke apart as the cop approached, shouting, "Driver—step out of the car slowly with your hands in the air!" He was standing to the rear of the car with his gun drawn. "Driver first! Step out of the car slowly!"

Rowe sat there trying to evaluate the situation, but could see that everything was finished.

"Driver! Open your door and put both arms out where I can see them, then step out of the car slowly! Do it *now*!"

Lofton eased the short barrel over the edge of his seat while the policeman was shouting. Rowe suddenly shifted gears and tried to floor it as Lofton fired at the cop through the rear window, in a near-simultaneous discharge with the officer's gun. The Firebird jumped the curb, bounced, and finally came to a stop when Lofton managed to throw it into park, hitting the dashboard.

The cop was down. Rowe was draped over the wheel. Lofton's ears were ringing as he flicked on the interior bulb and pulled his friend back by the shoulder, to see that he'd been shot in the head. His expression was empty, and the windshield was a mosaic of blood and matter from the exit wound.

Lofton was trembling as he turned the handle. He started to walk over to the officer lying on the street, but climbed back into the passenger side and cleaned the inside of the door with his T-shirt and jacket sleeve, then the dashboard and gear shift. After that he checked himself for blood spatter, and picked up the Ruger and wiped it before putting it back on the seat.

Now would probably be the time to distance himself from it. A skin follicle or something on the trigger could place him at the scene, but they didn't have his DNA as they did his prints. He couldn't remember holding the Glock.

He listened to the police frequency as wind blew down the empty road. The cop might have radioed for backup. He hurriedly wiped off the outer door handle and the edge of the roof, pondering the guns. They could still lead the police to O'Hara in theory, who'd sell him out, but he also had Marva's people to worry about.

Lofton pocketed the Ruger. He then went over and picked up the officer's Glock. Feeling its heft, he tried to find the safety before shoving it into his jacket. The cop, who had been shot in the chest, wasn't wearing a vest and was now unconscious if he was even alive. It didn't make much difference either way; if he hadn't radioed in the fact that he'd pulled over two individuals, the detectives were going to piece it together.

He collected the other Glock from the car, took a final look at Rowe, and began a tentative, stiff-legged jog in the direction of the smokestack to avoid traffic. The area was not only desolate but exposed, however: a long barren straightaway with nowhere to hide, and no access to a bus or a cab. He turned and went back towards Cherry. His leg bothered him, but it wasn't far to Lake Shore Boulevard and the Gardiner overpass; from there it was only a few blocks to the all-night King streetcar.

Lofton was sweating. He slowed to a laboured walk with a stitch in his side, looking away as an SUV drove past. It stopped ahead to make a left at the lights, the driver evidently unaware of the situation behind them on Commissioners.

When he was almost at the intersection, a cruiser suddenly rounded the corner in a wide turn, lights flashing, no siren. It was too late to hide, but they didn't seem to have noticed him. He watched the car over his shoulder as it sped down the road, braked, and hung an abrupt left. He started a limping run again. All the buildings on Cherry north of the expressway would more than likely be closed; he'd have a better chance surfacing in a more populated area, and found a bicycle path that was partially concealed behind bushes along the south side of the Lake Shore between a chain-link fence and grown-over railway tracks.

Making his way further west, he heard sirens. There was a terrain of broken concrete and gravel hills behind a cement manufacturer. Billboards stood along the north side close to the Gardiner, where bright signs on top of the old Gooderham Distilleries for Kahlua and Canadian Club reminded him that he needed a fucking drink. An unmarked car with a temporary light on its roof raced by on the far side of the foliage.

Traffic was light. Lofton waited behind a pillar by the guardrail at the bottom of Parliament for a solitary driver to stop for the signal. He heard another siren which might have been that of an ambulance, and was about to try to make it to King when a woman slowed to a stop in the westbound lane. He started running across the street with a gun drawn, but as soon as she saw him her Mazda lurched forward and then raced away.

Lofton put the Glock in his jacket and ran over to Parliament as two more cars pulled up, and another turned onto Lake Shore. The street ahead was nearly empty. There were sirens in the distance, one of which was getting louder as he walked under a railway trestle and up the east sidewalk close to the wall, nearly out of breath, looking for an alley. He stepped into the doorway of a rust proofing centre and watched a cruiser speed across an intersection a couple of blocks north, towards Cherry.

Walking past a construction site and auto dealership, Lofton saw an approaching car and ducked into a tiny park. It wasn't a cop. He ran to the middle of the road with his left hand up, aiming the Ruger at the driver. It still had two bullets. As the BMW came to a stop, he rushed over and gestured for the driver to get out. The man looked Italian, about fifty. He fumbled with his seat belt and opened the door.

"Hurry up!" Lofton shouted, looking around.

"What? What are you doing?"

Lofton grabbed him by the coat collar and tried to haul him out. When the driver was standing up, Lofton moved him around so that his own back was to the car, his gun pressed to the man's chest. He hesitated, and then fired. The driver made a half-strangled noise as he collapsed backwards onto the asphalt and lay writhing for a few seconds. Lofton watched him grow still and was about to feel for a pulse or shoot him again when he saw another car coming down the street behind him. He climbed behind the wheel, shifted gears, and started driving. He watched the vehicle in the mirror stop by the body, but rather than getting out, the driver suddenly accelerated.

Lofton barely slowed at the red light, and might have burned rubber if not for the BMW's grip on the road as he sped west on Lake Shore. The car behind him was an eight-cylinder boat, a Buick or something. They passed traffic going the opposite direction in the underpass. Lofton took the centre lane and shifted down, holding the wheel with his left hand, and tried to twist around, leaning out the window for a wild shot, but it was too difficult. The car's handling didn't allow for much give with the steering. He put the Ruger on the seat beside him and picked up one of the Glocks, turning the other direction to fire a volley of rounds through the rear window, which blew out much of the glass. The driver lost control and swerved into an abutment. Lofton heard the crash under the expressway as he shifted from third up to fourth again, and saw two other vehicles pull over. Now maybe there were no witnesses except the woman who got away.

As he passed Yonge Street he changed lanes and got onto the Gardiner ramp. With the rear window gone he didn't want to chance driving all the way home, and decided to head back to Marva's. Ditch the car as soon as he got off the Dunn Avenue exit, and walk over to Spencer.

It was 3:25. Adjusting the rearview mirror, he saw blood smeared on the side of his sweaty face and in his hair. As he reached for a cigarette he realized that he hadn't cleaned out the Firebird's ashtray. Even if they tried to match his DNA, however—and they would, Rowe having been the one to bail him out of jail—he wouldn't need to deny having been in his car.

Lofton turned on the radio, passing billboards, lights and an industrial landscape north of the railway tracks below. He was going to have to tell O'Hara what was going on, since he and Rowe worked together and the police were bound to question him as well. He'd swing by the house to brief him, or take him out altogether and tie up one big fucking loose end.

He turned off and continued along Adelaide—a spare, less-travelled route between old factories and warehouses on the edge of the garment district—then up to Queen. Shabby looking bookstores, textile outlets, coin laundries and furniture stores were interspaced with pastel-coloured restaurants and the odd gallery.

Driving along Euclid, Lofton was dismayed to see flashing lights on the road ahead, and realized that squad cars were parked near O'Hara's place. He turned into a driveway. There was a tremor in his leg as he backed out again, trying to keep it together.

23

Lofton was piecing it together as he drove past the old Palace Tavern on King. A neighbour might have heard O'Hara's shots and later called police after seeing them carrying out what looked like bodies. Such suspicions wouldn't have justified a warrant, however, and it was possible that the cops would have needed to persuade him to invite them inside if they had less than probable cause. But he wouldn't have been that stupid. Not that a few hours would make much difference if they really wanted to investigate.

They'd still have no victims, names or murder weapon, and it was possible that nobody would even file a missing persons report. But they'd eventually match the blood types or DNA to the corpses in the car, and a connection between Rowe and O'Hara would be easy enough to establish. After that, it would just be a matter of time before O'Hara identified him as the other triggerman in the bank. Lofton wasn't sure if O'Hara knew his last name or had any idea where he lived. Then he remembered the knife, which Rowe must have had on him in the car. But he hadn't touched it, so that wasn't a problem.

Lofton knew he had to get off the road as quickly as possible. Back to Marva's, then home in the morning to pick up his belongings, clear out his bank account before it was frozen, and split town. Go Stateside with his green card. Take a Greyhound to Buffalo, fly to California, and wait to show up on *America's Most Wanted* now that they were including Canada. He kept flashing on Rowe's expression at the wheel afterwards, as if he couldn't process having been shot through the head. And now he was on the run while

O'Hara, who was responsible for all this, was still alive to turn Crown witness.

Lofton drove over the crest of the hill and through the lights at Dufferin, past the closed bars, stores and Taco Bell. He steadied his speed and looked out the window. Parkdale always seemed to have the ugliest hookers.

At Spencer he turned left, looking for a place to park, and wondered how long it would take the police to start looking for the BMW. They'd identify the driver, but the car might take a while if the ownership and insurance were in the glove compartment. If he'd lifted his wallet it would have bought him some more time. What was a sharp-dressed wop in such a car doing down there in the middle of the night anyway? Maybe he had a body in the trunk too.

Lofton parallel parked between a Hyundai and a rusting K-Car, and wiped off his fingerprints. In this neighbourhood the odds were good that it was going to get scratched or have its decal pried off for a necklace. He walked up the street with his shoulder to the wind, his hand around the stock of one of the guns in his pockets as he tried to work out a strategy. Maybe Marva would come with him. He could sponsor her, or try to get her some fake ID. But of course it might be a problem being employed under his own name when there was obviously an extradition treaty between the U.S. and Canada. But one fucking thing at a time.

He walked up her driveway. The light was still on. At the bottom of her steps he tested her door handle with his left hand and found it unlocked. When he went in, a large motherfucker suddenly heaved himself up from the sofa and went for a gun on the coffee table. Lofton managed to thumb off the safety while he pulled out his Glock, which barely cleared his pocket when it discharged. The blast reverberated in the room as he tried to aim at the dodging man maneuvering with his own weapon, and fired again. The ex-boyfriend or whatever crashed into the TV as two others emerged from her bedroom and toilet with guns drawn, trying to stay out of one another's line of fire as Lofton shot at them blindly on his way out the door.

He got up the steps, looking back while he hurried down the driveway. They appeared, but quickly scrambled for cover as he shot at them repeatedly. When the clip was empty he did his best to run, reaching for another gun, but they returned fire. Bullets penetrated cars and shattered windows. Lofton was hit more than once, and fell down hard in the street as the Glock slid away along the asphalt. Tyrone sprinted over, followed by Rasheed. Marva screamed from the basement steps in her housecoat as he took careful aim and shot Lofton in the back of the head. "That's for Ice, *bitch*."

"What have you done?" She rushed down the driveway and knelt by Lofton, crying. "You killed him!"

Rasheed yanked on his toque as he looked around. "Yo, let's get Ice, man, and get out of here."

"Call an ambulance or something!" she wailed. "Help!"

"He fuckin' shot Ice and tried to kill *us*, ho." Tyrone turned and walked back to the house.

"Help! Police!"

"Shut the fuck *up*!" he yelled, going down the steps.

Marva stood up and started to run to a neighbour's, then stopped and went back to Lofton. "Help!" she cried, kneeling beside him. His blood was on her housecoat. She tried to turn him over and lift his head, then put him down and looked around, starting to get up again. "Call the police!"

A man five houses away was peering out his front door when they came back down the driveway with Ice propped up between them. "Call the *police*!" she yelled at him.

Rasheed held up the automatic and fired in that direction. The neighbour disappeared as windows broke and bullets ricocheted off brick and cement. Tyrone steadied himself with his left arm around Ice, and discharged a few rounds into Marva, who fell and lay sprawled in the road a few feet from Lofton.

They bundled the injured man onto the back seat, then climbed into the front. Their headlights went on as they pulled out into the street and made a wide U-turn over the curb and a front yard, heading south.

A Note On the Author

Among other things, Trevor Clark has worked as an oilrig roughneck, editor, portrait photographer, bookstore manager, and home entertainment coordinator for a TV movie production company in London, where he lived for a number of years. He is the author of *Born To Lose* (ECW Press, 1989,) *Dragging the River, Love On the Killing Floor*, and *Escape and Other Stories* (Now Or Never Publishing, 2009, 2010, 2012,) and his photographs have appeared in *Designs of Darkness: Interviews With Detective Novelists*, (Bowling Green University Popular Press, 1983,) and *Interviews With Contemporary Novelists* (Macmillan/ St. Martin's Press, 1986,) both by Diana Cooper-Clark, as well as *Ross Macdonald: A Biography*, by Tom Nolan, (Scribner's, 1999,) *NOW*, and *The Globe And Mail*. He is from Toronto, and currently lives in Vancouver.

ACKNOWLEDGEMENTS

My thanks to stellar publisher/editor, Chris F.
Needham. Also to Alison T., and Jack Higgins:
learned vagabond and master storyteller.